FEB 0 3 2010

THE SECRET OF HOLLY GREEN MANOR

Other books by Karen Cogan:

An Artful Deception
The Secret of Castlegate Manor
A Flame in the Wind
Stolen Dreams

THE SECRET OF HOLLY GREEN MANOR

•

Karen Cogan

AVALON BOOKS
NEW YORK

Published by Thomas Bouregy & Co., Inc.
160 Madison Avenue, New York, NY 10016

Library of Congress Cataloging-in-Publication Data

Cogan, Karen.
  The secret of Holly Green Manor / Karen Cogan.
     p. cm.
  ISBN 978-0-8034-9997-3 (acid free paper)
  1. Family secrets—Fiction.   I. Title.
  PS3603.O325S44 2010
  813'.6—dc22

                        2009027117

PRINTED IN THE UNITED STATES OF AMERICA
ON ACID-FREE PAPER
BY HADDON CRAFTSMEN, BLOOMSBURG, PENNSYLVANIA

Chapter One

Lydia Summers bent her head over the journal that contained her mother's last words. She was mildly surprised that her father had left it to yellow in a dusty black trunk in the attic. And yet, considering the circumstances, surely he would not like to be reminded of her sudden death. It was too cruel that she had been still young and full of life. Lydia's father had been right here with Mama, in this very spot, unable to stop her life from ebbing away. And he had never forgiven himself for not dying in her stead.

Lydia shivered as a cloud obscured the sun, blocking the light so that it no longer spilled through the garret window. Her lantern cast a glowing circle around her, leaving the rest of the attic in shadow. Vague forms of shrouded furniture and coffinlike

1

trunks lay witness to the many generations of Summerses who had lived in this house. Yet it was not their ghosts that haunted Lydia, for she barely remembered their names. She was haunted by the warning in her mother's journal. Mariah had been consumed by fear, fear for her husband and fear for the lives of a future generation. And yet the object of her fear escaped Lydia's understanding. She mentioned no names and left no clue as to how to unravel the mystery of her death.

Lydia remembered nothing of the fateful evening. She had been little more than an infant. Yet now, as she read her mother's words, she suspected that murder was the outcome. Why else would Mariah pen a warning, expressing a fear that a curse followed the family heirs?

In the journal, Mariah had reported her suspicions that a series of mishaps suffered by the household were deliberate attempts to harm her husband. She gave no hint that she had ever felt herself to be in danger. And then, on a late-fall afternoon, a day just like this one, a bullet had shattered the garret window, striking Mariah in the chest. She had died in this room where she had loved to sit alone and write in her diary.

Some said her death had been an accident. Nothing to the contrary had ever been proved. And yet, Lydia could not forget the suspicions that Mariah had expressed, suspicions that had been stilled that day, never to be expounded upon again.

Lydia curled her slender legs beneath her muslin day dress as she read:

There is always danger as long as there is greed in the world. And when one is an heir, one is the target of that greed. The women in this family have felt the pain of bereavement before, and I fear that I shall not escape the experience myself. I must find a way to protect Geoffrey and break this curse. Yet how may I do so when I do not know the enemy?

The account trailed off with a reference regarding the tragic history of Holly Green Manor. Dark secrets, murder, and betrayal plagued the descendants residing in the graceful old home. Mariah's last words had ended with the dark prediction that, until the secret was unraveled, there would be grave peril to those who dwelled in this house.

A gust of wind rattled the garret window. Lydia's lantern flickered. The shadows deepened, and a chill filled the room. Reluctant to move from her reading spot, Lydia lingered, cradling the journal in her hands. And though she felt closer to her mother here, she wished she might have known her. How different life would have been. She had felt it most keenly when she was away at school in London. Other girls met their mothers for visits to the dressmaker, for shopping and tea. And though her father provided her a generous pension to provide for her clothing, it did not take the place of a mother's companionship. So, on the occasions when she was invited along with her friends, she felt awkward and pitied. Finally, she declined the invitations altogether.

And now, having left school at last and returned to her childhood home, she could not believe how much she had missed the house and grounds. And she had missed the little mare she had ridden through the sweet-smelling pastures. Papa had often assured her in his letters that the groom was exercising her horse. And yet she had longed to return for more than two weeks at a time. She had missed the freedom of riding as often and as long as she liked.

School had been tedious and confining. She had chafed at the reprimands she received for her frequent withdrawal into her own imagination. The four years she spent there had seemed a lifetime. And when she boarded the carriage for home, she had left without a backward glance. She would miss the company of a few close friends but not the rigid schedule or book work that had sentenced her to long hours indoors on glorious spring days.

She remembered how she had longed for her first glimpse of home as the carriage clattered along the graveled drive. Very little had changed in her absence.

The small circular pond glittered like a diamond in the sunlight. The hedges along the lane lay trimmed into perfect cones. And the house had not changed at all. The gray turrets still rose to point skyward. The gray brick fascia rounded into a portico. And a dozen windows gleamed like glassy eyes to welcome her home.

Her father had been at home when she arrived. He had done his best to make her feel welcome. He had spent the afternoon with her, joining her for tea and listening to her account of receiving her diploma. She was both pleased and surprised by his effort. He had never been a large part of her life, often away on business and allowing her to be reared by her nanny.

She wondered if the distance that had existed between them was because she was a daughter instead of a son, and, thus, not an heir. Or, perhaps, she reminded him of her mother, and he found it painful to be with her, though it was certainly not in appearance that the similarity existed, for she was small and olive-skinned, while her mother had been tall, willowy, and fair.

As a child, she had spent hours staring at her mother's portrait, willing the young woman to step out of the confines of the canvas and come alive. She felt that, had her mother lived, they would have been a true family, the close family she had craved. And, yet it was not possible, and she knew it. So, when she lay in bed at night, she had begun to imagine finding the person responsible for killing her mother. Oh, how she longed to bring him to justice, to see him pay the price for robbing her of a mother. Yet as the years passed, her hope of such a discovery had faded. Now that she had found the journal, she intended to scour it for clues.

She wondered if delving into the past would somehow lure the killer. She was pondering this idea when the stairs leading to her solitary nest gave a creak. Lydia felt her heart race and her hands grow clammy. She chastised herself for letting her imagination run away with her. The fact that her mother was killed in this attic did not mean that she would meet a similar fate. And yet instinct drove her to extinguish the lantern and sit frozen in the darkness.

Her pulse refused to cease its rapid tempo until after the doorknob turned and Eve peered into the shadows. She was carrying a candle that lit her pale face in an unearthly glow. Yellow curls framed her temples, giving her the appearance of the angels Lydia had seen years ago when her nanny had taken her to a museum in Paris.

Lydia stared at her friend a moment before saying, "Whatever are you doing here?"

Eve peered around, seeking Lydia amid the shadows. "I might ask you the same thing. I came to see you. Your father said you were up here."

"Yes. He told me about the journal Mama had kept. I wanted to read it for myself."

"After all these years, you just found out about it?"

"Papa does not like to talk about her death. Somehow, I believe he blames himself."

Lydia stood up and stretched. Her eyes ached, and her back was stiff from leaning over. Time had ceased to exist while she devoured the pages that revealed her mother's thoughts and experiences since she married Papa and came to live at Holly Green Manor. One thing puzzled her exceedingly. There was never a mention of Lydia's birth. She knew that Mama had been married for some time before she was born. Surely an event anticipated for years would be worthy of some notation. While she was pondering this mystery, Eve took a step into the room. "It is cold up here. Bring the book down to the parlor, and let me take a look."

Lydia felt unsure about sharing the journal. Though Eve was a neighbor and had become a frequent companion since Lydia returned from school, their friendship seemed forced at times, as though Eve kept part of herself aloof. So it seemed only fair that Lydia be entitled to withhold her mother's personal thoughts from Eve. However, having told her about it, she could hardly refuse her curiosity now. Eve would be sure to sulk, and there was really nothing in the journal that would cause embarrassment or harm to Lydia's family if she allowed Eve to read it.

So she followed the golden-haired girl down the

steps to the candlelit hallway that led to the upstairs parlor. She held the journal against her heart as she paused in front of the door. Her slipper-clad toes dug into the plush Turkish rug that ran the length of the hallway. The bright scarlet threads against a background of amber were among her earliest memories. Before she had been allowed to ride, she had loved to play pony down the length of the hallway.

"Are you sure you want to see this? I fear you will find it tedious."

Eve gave her a sweet smile, her cornflower blue eyes fixed upon the book.

"I assure you that I will find it fascinating. Was there not a mystery surrounding your mother's death?"

"Yes. The assailant was never caught, nor the motive known for sure. Perhaps it was an accident."

"Perhaps. Ring for tea, and we shall see what your mama has written."

Lydia pulled the cord and then settled against the high, cushioned back of her chair. A fire glimmered merrily in the hearth. Lydia might have been cheered by its brilliant dance had she not been watching Eve so intently. With impeccable posture, Eve turned toward the light as she held the book in her lap, her slender fingers turning the delicate pages. Her blue gaze flickered across the pages, sometimes pausing to study a line or frowning a bit in concentration.

The tea arrived, and Lydia dismissed the young maid, saying, "I shall pour for us, Sarah. Thank you."

Eve sipped her tea distractedly. It seemed forever before she looked up from the journal and said, "Of course, I have not had time to examine it thoroughly, but from reading the last entry, I believe it must have been an accident. I think a hunter came too close to the house, and a stray bullet killed your mother. The hunter probably never knew what he had done."

Lydia frowned. "Perhaps. But did you not see the part about a long-standing feud regarding the inheritance of Holly Green Manor? It makes me wonder if someone planned a deliberate attack."

"What use would there be in killing your mother? It was your father who inherited the house."

Lydia shook her head. "You are right. Still, I cannot help but feel this was something deeper and more sinister than an accident."

Eve gave her head a superior shake. "That is the trouble with you, Lydia. You are always imagining more than is there. Remember last summer when you thought you saw someone riding away from your house at well past midnight?"

"Yes."

"Well, it must have been a dream or else an animal that you saw."

Lydia frowned. "That does not explain why our

pond was poisoned. If we had not found the dead ducks beside it, one of us might have died instead."

Eve sighed, obviously summoning her patience. "I am sure there is no connection, dear. One of the servants probably dumped lye into it."

Lydia took a sip of her tea, set the delicate rosebud cup back upon the saucer, and replied, "I suppose that's possible."

She decided to change the subject. She had long ago learned that it was fruitless to argue with Eve. When Eve made up her mind about a subject, there was simply no changing her view. This fact *did* change Lydia's opinions. In fact, it often made her more stalwart in her beliefs. Yet, to avoid argument, she simply refrained from letting Eve know that she remained unconvinced.

"Papa has just informed me that my cousin, Mr. James Summers, is planning a visit to the manor. We lost contact with him for quite some time. It seems his father bought a commission into the Army and moved to India. James commissioned into the Navy. He has just returned from serving under Lord Wellington. He is to inherit the estate upon Papa's death."

Eve pursed her thin lips and studied her teacup before saying, "I suppose he is dreadfully handsome, this cousin of yours."

"I do not know. I have never met him. There was a falling-out among my uncles, and they went their separate ways after my father inherited the estate."

Eve looked thoughtful. "And what will happen to you? I suppose you will be expected to marry Mr. Summers."

Lydia shuddered. "I should hope not. I will not marry a man I do not love, nor will I consent to a marriage of convenience."

"You had better be careful with those sentiments. You may become as poor as Reginald and I. Why, we barely have enough to get by on since Papa died and we moved here from London."

"But you and your brother are getting by, and that would be preferable to a loveless marriage or, worse still, one in which the partners came to despise one another. I believe my parents were very much in love; else my father would not have grieved all these years. Surely he will not attempt to persuade me, should I object."

Eve smiled. "I'm sure that you are right. I hope you will keep in mind that my brother, Reginald, holds you in high regard. When his station is improved, I hope that you may consider him as a suitor."

"Thank you. I shall remember."

In truth, Lydia had not found Reginald to her taste. Though he was a well-spoken young man, tall and blond and fair in appearance, on their few occasions of meeting she had found him prideful and condescending, though she could not imagine why he should be so. The house that they leased on the adjoining property was barely more than a cottage, certainly nothing at all compared to Holly Green Manor.

His eyes were just as blue as Eve's but held not a hint of mirth. She did not believe she had ever seen Mr. Reginald Smyth show even the slightest trace of a smile. With his dour nature, he could never fulfill her hope of one day residing in a house full of joy and laughter. She had grown up in a quiet and lonely environment, with a father who was pensive and often gone. She would not easily settle for an adulthood of the same. No, even if Mr. Smyth should amass a fortune in gold, she would not settle for him. Nor would she settle for her cousin, Mr. Summers.

Surely she was right, and Papa would not press her. She had not thought of marriage until Eve had brought up the possibility. Did everyone simply assume that she would marry in order to secure her future?

Eve persisted, "If you do not marry Mr. Summers, what will you do? You cannot stay here after your father passes on."

"Papa is in excellent health. It will be years before I have to think of it. By then I may have met and married a rich admiral." She added playfully, "If not, I shall hire myself out to you as a tutor, for I am sure you will have married quite well by then."

Eve frowned. "Joke if you like, but it is cunning

planning that keeps one in silks and lace. You may be surprised at the stature that Reginald and I shall attain."

Lydia looked into Eve's adamant gaze. "I am sorry. I did not mean to mock you. I will not be at all surprised if you and Reginald do very well for yourselves."

Eve nodded, and her blond curls bobbed. "We shall. And if you are smart, so shall you."

Lydia did not ask what she meant by the comment. To do so was to risk coming full circle to the subject of Mr. Summers and the sensibility of marriage. She would meet the man soon enough and was already fully prepared to dislike him. It would not surprise her in the slightest to discover, upon his arrival, that he was engaged to some covetous young girl who could not wait for Papa to die so that they could evict her and move onto the estate.

As Lydia dwelled upon that unhappy thought, Eve announced that it was time for her to be off.

"Reginald said that he would call 'round for me at six o'clock. He is always prompt."

Eve took a last sip of tea before rising. She rang for her cloak and then accompanied Lydia from the fire-lit room to the shadowy hallway. Their shadows rose and fell as they trod in candlelight down the foyer.

The young maid, Sarah, brought Eve's cloak.

A moment later a knock sounded upon the door. She opened it to find Mr. Reginald standing upon the stoop. He bowed and doffed his top hat to Lydia. "Good evening, Miss Summers. We are in for a chilly night, I believe."

Lydia shivered from the draft of the wind as well as his formal manner and icy blue eyes.

Reluctantly she gathered her manners and said, "I believe you are right, sir. Will you not come in and warm yourself before you are off?"

"I think not, though I thank you for your kind offer and for entertaining my sister while I was in town. I fear we are about to have snow, and I wish to get the horses home before there are any drifts."

Lydia nodded, feeling secretly relieved. Eve's visit had already kept her from the journal, and she wished to peruse it a bit further before supper. She bid them a polite good-bye and turned eagerly for the parlor. She could not help but think that, had she not been the only young woman within easy visiting distance, Eve would not have sought her as a friend. Eve was ambitious, all her thoughts centering upon improving her station, an accomplishment that interested Lydia not at all. It was not position that Lydia prized but rather true friendship and companionship with genial and like-minded friends. And for her part, she did not always find Eve to be a jolly companion.

Secured in her chair, she stretched her toes toward

the fireplace, warming her thin slippers as she scoured the journal, looking for any clues she might have missed. At last she shut it with a sigh. She was no closer to finding out the truth about her mother's death than when she had begun. Instead, she was plagued by unanswered questions and the suspicion that foul play had been afoot.

A glance at the mantel clock gave her a start. It was much later than she realized, nearly time for supper, and Papa did not like to be kept waiting. Taking the journal with her, she flew up the stairs and hurried through a change of dress. Smoothing her dark curls into submission, she arrived downstairs just in time to be seated with her father.

"I am sorry I was very nearly late. I have been reading Mama's journal. Though she wrote it so many years ago, reading it makes me feel as though I am there with her, hearing her speak her thoughts to me. Thank you for allowing me to know her better."

He studied her solemnly for a moment. She noticed that his pale strands of hair were thinning and his eyes were a lighter blue than the portrait of him as a young man. She was not a suspicious person, so why did she suddenly fear that reading the journal would somehow put him in danger? Was it because Eve had spoken of his future demise? Whatever the reason, she was suddenly filled with the fear of losing him.

She studied him. Had he always been so thin? He

had been tall and slender ever since she could remember. Yet in the last few years it seemed he had
grown gaunter. She looked at the ample portions of
pheasant and baked pears, potatoes and pastry upon
the sideboard and knew that he would only sample a
small portion of each, hardly enough to keep the flesh
on his tall frame.

He sighed and said, "It pains me to think of your
mother's journal and how abruptly it ended. And yet
I believe it is only fair that you have something of
her, something that you may know her by."

Lydia nodded. "I have always missed her. Even
though I do not remember her voice or her touch, I
know she was a wonderful mother."

They drifted into their own thoughts as the butler served the succulent pheasant. The aroma of the
meat and rich gravy teased her senses, yet Lydia was
hardly aware of her hunger. She stared at the pol-
ished cherry wood table that gleamed under the soft
light of the chandelier and imagined how different
their meals would be if her mother were alive.
Judging from the writing in the journal, Lydia believed that Mariah had been a vibrant and passionate person, someone who would liven conversation
and brighten her father's stodgy moods.

"Eat your supper, daughter. Your food will grow
cold."

Lydia glanced up at her father to see his disap-
proving gaze upon her plate. Obediently she took a

bite of meat. She chewed thoughtfully, then asked, "I understand that there was a quarrel in the family, long ago, about the inheritance of Holly Green Manor. How did it begin?"

He grimaced in distaste. "I hate to speak of it. If it is true, it does not put our family in a good light."

Lydia met the gaze of his blue eyes with a pleading furrow of her brow. "Please. I really want to know, to understand the reason my mother may have been murdered."

Geoffrey Summers set down his fork with a sigh. "It began when your great-uncle died, leaving a daughter but no son to inherit. His daughter, Cassandra, insisted that his nephew had murdered him, but there was no proof. She felt ill-treated when your grandfather inherited the estate and she was left to survive by becoming a governess."

Lydia leaned forward, shocked by such an awful possibility.

"You do not think that Grandfather killed him?"

"I surely don't want to think it. It is a dreadful thought."

"Surely it could not be so—your very own father."

Geoffrey shook his head. "No, indeed it couldn't be true. He was a highly ambitious man and managed the estate shrewdly. He was harsh on the tenants, believing they would be lazy if not forced to suffer the consequences of a poor yield, even if nature was the reason. And yet I believe his motive was always to provide for the security of his family."

Lydia frowned. "How did all of this involve Mother? Her death could not remove you from inheritance."

"I have pondered that myself. I can think of only two reasons, one of which was to keep me from fathering a son, who would inherit. The second was that I was the intended target, and she was killed by mistake."

"But who would do such a thing, so many years later?"

Geoffrey ran a hand through his thinning hair. "Cassandra died several years ago. Before she passed away, she penned a bitter note to me vowing that her descendants would one day reside in this house. I have lost track of her children. And there has been no more violence since your mother was killed. I can only believe that Cassandra was somehow behind it. Perhaps she felt vindicated by Mariah's death."

Lydia puzzled through the relationships and said, "My cousin who is to arrive is the son of your younger brother. He is next to inherit the estate. Perhaps the killer has been waiting for him to appear. After all, there is nothing to gain by killing either of us."

Geoffrey frowned at his daughter. "I think you have been overly influenced by the journal. Therefore, I forbid that you express your fanciful notions to your cousin. He will think you are cracked."

"They are not fanciful, Papa. If you think about it, it makes perfect sense."

"Then I command you not to think about it. I intend for Mr. Summers to have a pleasant visit and then to go away. Do you understand?"

"Yes, but would it not be best to warn him? Perhaps he does not know the story of Cassandra's threat."

"Indeed, I see no reason to say a word. The threat was buried along with a bitter old woman. You will say nothing of it."

Lydia stared dumbfounded at Geoffrey's face, which had reddened to match the scarlet wine in his glass. She had rarely seen him agitated and was surprised to see him become so emotional. She bit back any further argument for fear that he would make himself sick.

"Of course, Papa, if you think it best, I will be all that is amiable with Mr. Summers, and I will not vex him by bringing up the past."

Geoffrey let out a breath, obviously relieved by her assurance. As the rush of color faded from his cheeks, he said, "I believe we need tolerate Mr. Summers for only a few days. I do not believe he plans to stay long."

Lydia frowned, surprised that her father did not

eagerly embrace the obvious solution to her future. Eve had certainly grasped it quickly. Surely he saw the obvious match between herself and the heir of the estate.

She took a sip of wine and said, "Why do you wish him to go away so quickly? Eve suggested that a marriage between Mr. Summers and myself would secure my future as mistress of the estate. I am sure you have thought of this. Do you not wish it?"

"Do you think me so indifferent as to have neglected thoughts of your future? Indeed no. I have thought of it long and hard. I do not believe such a marriage is in your best interest. After all, he is only a sailor. You will have a gentleman for a husband and not settle for less."

He spoke as though the matter was settled. Yet Lydia noticed that his hand shook as he lifted his goblet. Though they had never been as close as she would have liked, she knew him well enough to know that his behavior was strange. After all, if she had understood correctly, Mr. Summers was an officer and not merely a sailor. And it was not as though she was a titled woman likely to land a viscount or even a baron. She would most likely have to be content with a country gentleman with a modest estate.

She puzzled over her father's objection but did not trouble him with further questions. After all, she should have been relieved that he did not expect her to marry the heir of the estate. Though she had no intention of doing so, she would have understood his desire to have a direct descendent remain in the house. And though she loved her home dearly, she would rather remain unattached, spending her entire life as a governess than to marry for any reason except love.

They finished their meal in thoughtful silence and parted right afterward. Geoffrey excused himself to his library for brandy and a pipe, while Lydia trod the stairs to her chambers, engulfed in her thoughts. All around her, she was reminded of the comfort and richness of her life. The house was adorned with the finest woods and tapestries. Gilded decorations on the wall moldings, and velvet curtains on the windows contributed to a beautiful home of which to be proud. She had enjoyed a life of ease here, never hungry or cold or lacking for anything. And yet it could easily become a prison if she shared it with the wrong man.

While she wished she could unravel the secrets of the past, she had no desire to involve herself with Mr. Summers to do so. She had promised Papa to stay silent on the subject, and she intended to give it her best effort. Besides, what warning did she owe Mr. Summers, a man so crass as to intrude into her home to assess what would one day be his?

She felt her anger rise against him. How could

anyone believe she would consider a man who would come poking around before Papa's demise? On that point, she could ease Papa's concern regarding a marriage. She would never consider marrying such a man. Papa could be assured of that.

Chapter Two

Two days later, Lydia had grown weary of the chilly, whistling wind that seeped in her windows. She was tired of glancing out at the dreary clouds that filled the sky. Too many hours indoors had left her sluggish and restless. Her patience with the satin coverlet she was embroidering grew thin, and she decided that a stroll along the hedges would awaken her mind and freshen her spirits.

She bundled into her heavy cloak of dusty rose and added a thick woolen scarf. Then, after pulling on her gloves, she set out to face the bitter wind of the frosty November afternoon.

On impulse, she stopped at the kitchen to collect some dry crusts of bread from Cook, who was busy with dinner preparations and willing to fetch the bread just to get her from underfoot. Perhaps the ducks who were visiting the pond now that the water was clean again would be happy to see her.

She walked along the gravel lane, following the hedges that lined it, enjoying their fragrant scent and their deep green against the barren backdrop of leafless trees that looked like skeletal silhouettes against the gray of the sky. Winter had never been her favorite season, just a necessity to get through in order to enjoy the freshness of spring.

She sighed. It would be weeks before the first signs of spring. And it would often be too wet for rides across the meadows. She would have to content herself with short walks to make up for the monotony of spending so much time indoors.

She felt sure that most of her old school friends were looking forward to the holiday season in London. Their debuts were often discussed and eagerly anticipated as they prepared to leave the academy. But the ensuing preening and incessant parties held no appeal for Lydia. She hoped that Papa would not suggest they go. Since he had never been one to enjoy social affairs, he would be going entirely on her behalf. And while it would be a noble gesture, she had no desire to be paraded about in lace and other frippery in the hopes of attracting the richest possible suitor.

She was so completely engrossed in her thoughts that she did not hear the coach that careered toward her just around the bend in the lane. With a shriek of alarm, she shrank against the bushes to escape its lumbering bulk. She stared, wide-eyed, as it passed her and continued along toward the house. Only the briefest view of the occupant's bright blue eyes was possible, yet she registered their shock to see her wedged against the bushes.

Inside the coach, James Summers sucked in his breath to see a young woman so narrowly escape disaster. Even though he had time for only a passing impression, her visage was irrevocably implanted in his mind. Her large dark eyes had stared in stunned surprise from a heart-shaped pixie face that was becomingly framed by her bonnet. Even bundled into a heavy cloak, it was obvious that she was petite.

He leaned out the window to stare behind him. What was she doing walking the lane on such a chilly afternoon? Perhaps she was a serving girl sent on an errand. He could think of no other explanation, for she was surely no kin to his tall, blond, Plantagenet ancestors.

Even so, she was a pretty minx, and he was glad she had not come to harm. He would ask Uncle Geoffrey about her and make his apologies to her mistress for the near collision. Perhaps he would even see the girl again as she went about her duties. He did not find the thought unpleasant, for he could not forget the deep brown of her eyes, opened wide with alarm like those of a startled deer. He suspected she was a timid creature, used to serving in obscurity. He hoped she bore no ill effects from the near mishap.

For Lydia's part, anger had begun to replace her initial surprise. How dare this man, whoever he might be, round the curve as though he owned the manor, nearly plowing her down? If she had been a foot nearer the center of the lane, she would not be alive to tell about it.

She glared at the receding coach. Her desire for a walk had evaporated, replaced by an urgent desire to discover the identity of the occupant. She had not recognized either the man or the coach. Suddenly it struck her. It must be young Mr. Summers, come for a perusal of the manor. If he meant to impress them with pomp and a fine coach, he would be sorely disappointed. She disliked him already, and they had not even met. And though she had promised Papa to be civil, an excuse to give him a good tongue-lashing would suit her very well.

As she stalked toward the manor, she was hardly aware of the bite of the wind as it lashed her cheeks. Dusk was falling, and her path was further obscured by an inky veil of clouds that hid the moon. Lightning flashed in the east, and she felt a drop of rain hit her nose.

Pulling her skirts above her ankles, she hurried to the shelter of the portico. Her pulse pounded from

her quick dash to the house as well as the strong ani-
mosity she felt. She took a deep breath to compose
herself before opening the door to the blessed still-
ness and warmth of the marbled hallway. She caught
sight of herself in the mirror that hung upon the mar-
ble pillar directly facing the door and frowned at her
image.

Her ribands had come untied and were strung
across her shoulders. Her nose was rosy from the
cold. The fringe that she had arranged upon her forehead had turned to tangled curls, and her scarf lay
crooked about her neck. She was hardly a picture of
dignity.

As she debated upon the prudence of slipping up
to her chambers before facing her guest, the butler
approached. He took note of her appearance and
managed to convey his disapproval by a slight tilt of
his head. "Your father is seeking you, miss. He de-
sires your presence in the drawing room."

Lydia summoned her dignity.

"Very well, Gaines. Take my damp wrap, and I
shall join him."

She handed her cloak and bonnet to Gaines and
drew herself to her full height, wishing she were tall
like Eve instead of small as a church mouse. But
never mind her size. She could be forceful when the
occasion demanded, and she was determined not to
tolerate any airs put forth by Mr. Summers.

A plush Asian rug, swirled in pink and soft blues,

lined the hall. She trod it silently, her damp slippers leaving an imprint as she approached the drawing room. She heard the men's voices and paused in the doorway. Her father and the stranger were standing near the massive fireplace at the opposite end of the room. Upon catching sight of her, they ceased their conversation. And as she caught her first good view of their visitor, she froze in consternation.

The young man who faced her looked nothing like the villain she had expected. He had a pleasant face that showed a dimple in his chin as he smiled at her. He stood a few inches taller than her father, giving him considerable height. His broad shoulders were neatly set off by a fine gray woolen riding coat, powder blue waistcoat, and fine white cravat. His pants fit tightly, showing the outline of his trim, muscular legs. Yet, most distressing of all was the look of approval in his striking blue eyes.

Feeling discomfited, Lydia entered the room.

Her father seemed less than pleased with her damp and disheveled appearance.

"I have had the house turned upside down looking for you. You cannot have been out on a night so wretched as this."

Lydia caught her lower lip with her teeth, still keenly aware of Mr. Summer's gaze.

"I am afraid that I was. I had no idea that the weather would turn foul before I could return."

Geoffrey shook his head. "Lydia, I would like to

introduce you to your cousin, Mr. James Summers. Mr. Summers, my daughter, Lydia."

Lydia bestowed a very formal curtsey as Mr. Summers bowed.

He studied her and said, "Why, you are the young woman my driver nearly plowed down in the lane. I am most terribly sorry. It gave me a dreadful scare on your behalf. I planned to apologize as soon as I reached the house. I had no idea that it was my very own cousin."

Lydia's brow wrinkled into a frown. "Indeed. Well, it could have been avoided if you had not been careering heedlessly along the lane."

A mild glimmer of amusement flickered in his eyes. "You are right, of course. I can only defend myself with the explanation that my driver was trying to get the horses to shelter before the storm. It would seem that you were not so fortunate as to escape the downpour."

Lydia felt her ire rise that he would dare tease her about her damp appearance. He might indeed be the most handsome man she had ever beheld, but that gave the cheeky devil no privilege of familiarity. If he were not kin, and the heir as well, she would demand his immediate departure. As it was, she would tolerate his presence and try to ignore his ability to stir her emotions.

She forced a smile. "As there was no permanent damage, I shall accept your apology and welcome you to Holly Green Manor. I hope that you find it suitable and to your taste."

"Indeed. I have liked what I have seen very much. There was little of beauty aboard the ship, and I am glad to be back upon land."

The sincerity of his smile took her quite off guard. When his gaze lingered upon her face, assessing every curve of her cheeks and lips, a flush crept to her cheeks. If he intended to flatter her, she would have to raise her guard. Her years at school had not left her entirely naïve. Just because he did not seem a cad did not mean he would not prove to be one. She would not fall prey to his charms, only to be cast aside like a worn saddle blanket when he took possession of the house.

She took a seat near the fire, upon the settee, and the men settled upon plush, rose-colored chairs on either side of her. Lydia pursed her lips and stared at the huge round log that glowed with red embers. It reminded her of her temper that, once aroused, was slow to die down.

She listened as Papa asked Mr. Summers, "I trust you had a good trip?"

"I did. We stopped briefly for food and ale upon the way and to stretch our legs. When we continued on, I had a chance to view the countryside. Having spent most of my life in the bustle of India, I believe that the tranquility of the manor life would suit me very well. My father passed away a year after my commission into the Navy, so when I retired, I came to London to the house that we previously owned there. Yet now there is nothing to hold me in London. I am thinking of selling my house and finding a house to let in your lovely countryside."

"Our countryside?"

Lydia could not keep her voice from rising. She had thought to have him as a brief guest at the manor and then be rid of him until the sad occasion of her father's death. Now it seemed he would settle nearby and await Papa's demise like a spider awaiting his next meal. That, she could not abide. Even if she rarely saw him, just knowing that he lay in wait would be intolerable.

Unwittingly encouraged by her question, young Mr. Summers launched into an animated account of his enthusiasm for the country and his determination to visit the nearby village and determine if there were any houses to rent.

"Why, if we were neighbors, I could come by now and again and get to know you both so much better. It would seem that you are the only family I have left, at least that I am aware of. Father rarely spoke of family. I believe there was an unfortunate rift at one time, one that I earnestly hope to repair."

He seemed so sincere that Lydia had to fight against her inclination to believe him. After all, what did she and Papa know of him? Only that he stood to inherit and that he had been reared on the family grudge. For all she knew, he could have come to hurry Papa's demise.

That terrible thought caused her to study his finely etched profile as she tried to decide if he looked to be the sort of man who would murder in order to fulfill his ambitions. After a few moments he glanced at her and raised his eyebrows at the intensity of her scrutiny. Lydia quickly looked away, becoming intent upon the lace that edged the cuff of her dress.

She was relieved when the maid brought tea and set it upon the small ivory table with carved legs that sat beside the settee. Lydia dismissed the girl and embraced the task of pouring the tea. It kept her attention focused and her eyes off of the perplexing Mr. Summers. Though she was aware of the lull in conversation as Papa and Mr. Summers awaited their tea, her thoughts were flitting like butterflies over what had caused the family rift.

She was conscious of Mr. Summers' brilliant blue eyes following her every move. And when their fingers brushed as she handed over his cup, she was surprised by the warmth of his hand. She had expected it to be as cold as she thought his heart to be.

He gave her a charming smile and asked, "Have you a liking of the country, Miss Summers?"

"Yes. I must say that I like it very much. Ever so much more than London, where I went to school. I enjoy long rides, and the air is much cleaner here."

Mr. Summers nodded. "I know what you mean.

Though I lived in London only as a young child, I do not remember liking it. I find now that the burning of so much coal by so many makes a great deal of grime."

After a moment's hesitation he said, "Perhaps we might all take a ride together one day. I would love to see the grounds."

Lydia bit back a bitter reply and said mildly, "But of course. You are the eventual heir. It is only natural that you would wish to inspect the holdings."

Taken aback, Mr. Summers creased his brow. "I did not think of it in those terms. I simply thought a ride would be pleasant, and I do admit to a curiosity about the home that my father spoke of so fondly."

"Was he bitter not to inherit?" Lydia asked.

The elder Mr. Summers shook his head. "That is hardly a proper question, my dear Lydia."

Young Mr. Summers met her direct gaze and answered without the slightest hesitation. "I do not mind. I hardly think my father gave it a thought. He was not much younger than your father and did not expect to inherit within his lifetime."

Lydia noticed that Papa kept a warning eye upon her as he shifted the conversation to a more tactful subject. "I hear that there are good riding trails in Hyde Park."

"It is true, though I have had no chance to enjoy them since my return. However, before I went aboard ship, I spent numerous hours riding the hills of India with the other young men. I had a fine roan that helped me win many a race."

Unbidden, the image of Mr. Summers racing along the wilds of India, as untamed as the land, invaded Lydia's mind. He would look fine upon a horse, his tall, slim frame resting gracefully in the saddle, a lock of thick blond hair falling over his brow. And though he had been born a gentleman, a stature such as his would make him look a gentleman no matter what his station in life.

He reminded her of a Roman statue she had once seen in London. He shared the aristocratic nose, chiseled face, and firm chin so admired in the statue. It was a confident, cheerful face, lacking in harsh lines. And his brilliant Plantagenet-blue eyes were enough to capture the heart of any maiden, excepting herself. She dared not allow his good looks to divert her from her suspicions. If he were here to harm them, she must discover his plan before it was too late.

They finished their tea, whereupon Papa suggested that Mr. Summers might like to spend some time in his room before they dined. When he expressed his appreciation, an upstairs maid was summoned to lead him to his accommodations. He bowed deeply and said, "I shall anticipate our reunion at supper. There is so much that I wish to know about your lives here at Holly Green Manor."

Lydia's suspicions rose. Perhaps he intended to

study their habits in order to see how to best dispose of Papa. If he proved to be the vile man she suspected, he might be using his charming good looks to catch them off guard. She shuddered. It was going to be insufferable to have him living in their house. She could not wait until he obtained a home of his own.

These thoughts weighed heavily upon her mind as she waited for him to disappear from the room. Then she turned to Papa and said, "I believe he has come to wreck ruin upon us. He stands to inherit if you are out of the way. Men of this family may already have murdered once to attain what they wanted. What is to keep Mr. Summers from doing so again?"

"After seeing how he studied you, I do not believe that is his intent at all. There is more than one way of attaining residence in this house. I do not believe he would be at all opposed to succeeding by way of marriage."

Lydia raised her eyebrows in surprise. "Would you now wish me to marry him?"

"No, indeed. The less you have to do with this young man, the better I shall like it. I could not bear to have you end as your mother did."

"I shall not. Before long I will get to the bottom of all of this—you shall see."

Papa shook his head. "Stay out of it, Lydia. I do not believe I am in any danger from Mr. Summers."

He stirred from his chair. "Now I shall go to my chambers for a rest before supper. I suggest that you do the same."

She did not argue about danger from Mr. Summers, but neither did she change her plans. She followed Papa upstairs and parted for her own chambers. She shivered as she lit her lamp. Though her fireplace had been lit to warm the room, it had yet to dispel the dampness that penetrated to her bones.

She pulled her curtains aside and stared out, watching the lightning flash through the swirling turmoil of dark clouds. Her mind felt as unsettled as the weather. How could she assure Papa's safety? If Mr. Summers had truly taken a fancy to her, it might be prudent to encourage his attentions. After all, if he were to believe her to be agreeable to marriage, he might postpone more dangerous plans in favor of residence at the estate.

Turning from the window, she bit her lower lip and studied the heavy mahogany furniture that had been in the family for decades. If only these walls, these furnishings could talk, she could unravel the history of murder that plagued this house. She dismissed it as a silly thought and picked up her mother's journal. She opened it to the beginning as she settled upon her bed and pulled the heavy white chenille coverlet to her chin.

On such a stormy night, it was easy to believe that envy and greed had led to murder. As she scanned the fine, thin lines of her mother's script, she became aware of the steady progression of anxiety. Over time, her mother's outlook changed from that of a happy, carefree bride to someone filled with a nervous suspicion that pervaded her every thought. And yet Mariah could hardly be accused of imagining the danger that had led to her death.

Lydia bit her lip, wondering again if Mr. Summers posed a threat. Until she knew the answer, she intended to keep careful track of his whereabouts. The servants would be useful in this regard if she could think of a believable story to cover the truth. She knew how some of them liked nothing better than a bit of intrigue. Permission to spy on a guest would be a delicious diversion to their days.

She fell asleep, still pondering what to tell them, until she was awakened by a light rap upon her door.

The newly arrived guest at the manor did not sleep while ensconced in his room. Instead, he sat at the desk in the well-appointed chamber and penned a letter that he would deliver to town in person on the morrow, for he did not trust its care to a servant. He sealed the letter and sat back in his chair, listening to the rumbling thunder and watching the fire flicker in the grate. He was pleased by what he had seen of the house. The current lord and his daughter had done well by it.

Someday he would inherit this manor and all of

the grounds. The thought should have excited him. And it would have done so if he had not been perplexed by the behavior of the fiery Miss Summers. Though obviously well-bred, she had not hesitated to dress him down for the near miss with the coach. Her dark eyes had sparked with anger when they first met and then, after his apology, had simmered during the remainder of their encounter.

He stretched his long legs toward the fire and wondered if she would be more agreeable during supper. She had seemed determined to dislike him, though he could never remember having met her before or giving her reason to think ill of him. Perhaps it was the inheritance that bothered her so. It would be only natural that she would be fond of her home. She would be displeased to have a stranger perusing it. Women set great store in their position as mistress of the house. She could not know that he had no intent of turning her out. He had made no attachments all the while that he served in the Navy. And he had come now with the intent of asking for her hand, should she prove an agreeable sort. He had never expected to start off with a black spot against him.

A smile crept across his face. He liked a challenge, and he liked a woman with spirit. Perhaps Miss Summers was just what he needed to help him forget about the battles that lay behind him. Instead, he could concentrate on the battle ahead. Since she seemed to resent his presence, he would remain for only a few days, just long enough to find a nearby home to rent. When he had settled in, he would make it a habit to call upon Miss Summers. And maybe, if he were lucky, he might win a friendship with his comely cousin.

Groggy with sleep, Lydia heard the upstairs maid telling her that it was nearly time for supper. She forced herself to rouse and tell the girl to come in. And then she came fully awake as she remembered the presence of Mr. Summers. She would face him at supper in less than a half hour.

She thought carefully about what she should wear. She did not want him to be misled into believing them to be unsuspecting and unsophisticated fools, easy targets for a man who wished them harm.

With that in mind, she had her girl fetch the royal blue damask, puffed at the shoulders with sleeves that narrowed to her wrists. She liked the effect of the modest bodice and straight skirt. And when her dark hair was piled atop her head and laced with the blue silk ribbons she had purchased in London, the ensemble gave the impression of more height than she actually possessed.

She sighed as she dismissed Sarah and shut the door to her chamber. Her slippers made no sound upon the plush carpet as she trod downstairs. She heard voices in the parlor and knew the men were waiting for her. She chewed her lower lip, feeling on edge as she prepared to encounter the man she hoped was not to become a dangerous adversary.

Mr. Summers was in the room, having a drink with Papa. Lydia shot him a suspicious glance as she joined them. In return, Mr. Summers gave her a slow, approving smile that sent color racing to her cheeks. She forced herself to maintain her gaze as she bestowed a guarded greeting.

"Good evening, Mr. Summers. I trust that your rest has refreshed you from your journey."

"Indeed it has. I am quite refreshed and most eager to deepen my acquaintance with my uncle and my charming cousin. It has been a long time since I have enjoyed such intriguing company."

She puckered her forehead. Was there a challenge behind his words? Did he think he would win her good favor? So far she had maintained her distance. If he wished to close that distance, he would have to convince her of his innocence regarding the estate.

If he did so, they could become friends, even if they did not wed.

He offered her his arm, and in spite of her intentions, she enjoyed his pleasant warmth as they followed her papa into the dining room.

There upon the sideboard lay an array of sauces and roasted meats. Bowls of boiled potatoes and stewed vegetables were spaced between the meats. Lydia felt her stomach rumble. She knew James must be hungry also, as it must have been hours since his last meal. Perhaps his mouth watered as hers did as she inhaled the aroma of the hearty fare.

James took the chair across from her, seeming delighted that he was to have an easy view of her expressions throughout the meal. Papa sat to his right at the head of the table and nursed the glass of port that he had begun in the parlor.

Lydia had been right about his appetite. James quickly found that his ravenous appetite quite outstripped that of his host. And while he tried to contain himself so as not to appear gluttonous, he still managed to work his way through several courses of food. And though his host ate little, it seemed he had a hearty appetite for information regarding James' past. He peppered James with questions. And though he became more animated after draining his third glass of wine, his grim expression softened.

"You must tell me about my dear brother. I suppose Richard told you about our childhood. We got along well, save an occasional quarrel or tussle. I was the elder, and Papa expected me to be serious and intent upon learning to manage the tenants and the manor. Richard was the one allowed to be lighthearted and carefree. I sometimes envied him the position of second son."

"I am sure that he envied you also. He loved this place. I believe that is why he moved us to India when I was only an infant. Mama died of fever there, leaving the two of us to manage alone. After he retired from duty, we returned to London, and Papa invested his savings. I joined the Navy and was on board ship when he died. I will always regret not being at his side."

In spite of her reticence, Lydia felt moved by his account. Surely a man who mourned his father could not be so heartless as to cause grief to another man's child. He seemed so sincere that she hardly knew what to make of him.

When they arose from their meal, Geoffrey was unsteady from too much wine and too little food. He smiled weakly and said, "I am afraid the excitement of having a guest has enticed me to indulge myself too deeply. I shall have to beg off and retreat to my chambers. Perhaps Lydia will consent to join you for coffee in the drawing room before you retire."

James nodded. "I should be delighted to have the company of Miss Summers."

Geoffrey shuffled toward the door. "Then I shall say good night until the morrow."

Lydia watched him, a frown upon her rosy lips.

"I hope he will feel himself in the morning," James said.

She shook off her concern and said, "I am sure he shall. It is not like him to become tipsy."

James offered his arm and led her back to the parlor. The butler brought steaming coffee, and Lydia was grateful for the warmth as she embraced the cup with her chilled fingers. She took a sip, watching James above the rim of her cup.

He smiled at her. "Will you not tell me about your childhood? There is so much I want to know."

Lydia studied him, trying to gauge his motive as she decided just how much she was willing to tell.

Chapter Three

Lydia peered at Mr. Summers over her delicate china cup and studied the intense interest in his blue eyes. She owed him nothing, yet perhaps cooperation would be the best way to win his confidence and encourage him to reveal more than he intended.

She forced a smile and said, "I recall only snippets of my earliest childhood. I do not remember my mother at all. I spent my girlhood with a nanny and then a governess until I was old enough to attend school in London. I have only recently arrived back."

"If you do not mind my asking, what did happen to your mother? My father alluded only to a tragic accident."

"La. That is what some would like to believe. It is

my firm conviction that she was murdered. There are dark secrets in this family that some would keep concealed. Do you know nothing of them, Mr. Summers?"

He frowned, knitting his fair eyebrows together. "I must confess that I do not. What was to be gained by the murder of your mother?"

She hesitated. She had promised Papa not to tell. Yet what would be gained by her silence? Feeling justified, she plunged ahead. "It is my belief that the bullet was intended for my father. Someone wanted this estate enough to be willing to murder for it. I believe the danger still exists, and I will not rest until I discover who was behind it."

"But that must have been well over fifteen years ago, about the time we moved to India. How shall you go about unraveling the crime?"

"It was eighteen years ago, to be exact. I shall not reveal my plans just yet, but you may be assured that they exist."

James shook his head. "I hope that you succeed, for your own peace of mind. Yet, even if it is true about the murder, I am sure the perpetrator has long fled the scene."

"Perhaps. But I shall stay alert nonetheless, as I have reason to believe, from my mother's journal, that the curse has not yet been lifted."

There. She had laid it out in the open. From James'

own admission, his father had packed them off to India soon after Mama died. Was it not likely that Richard's shame of failure and fear of discovery had caused him to flee? And now his son had returned. No doubt he was made of the same fiber. She cast him a covert glance.

James did not reply but seemed to puzzle over her words.

At last he said, "How good it is that your mother kept a journal. At least you have some way of knowing her. My mother died when I was very young also. I have no such comfort to which to turn."

Lydia stared at him. What a strange man. Did he really hope to throw her off guard by speaking sentimentally about his mother? And yet his expression looked so genuinely bereft that, if it were not sincere, she could only applaud his skill in acting.

She finished her coffee and said, "It is late, Mr. Summers, and you must be tired. I shall retire to my chambers and allow you to do the same."

He nodded. "You shall join us on the ride tomorrow, shall you not?"

Her dark eyes narrowed in warning. "I shall. You may count upon it."

She turned without another word and left him alone beside the fire. If he thought that she would send him to ride alone with Papa, he was mistaken. All sorts of "accidents" could be arranged during the course of a morning ride. And she had no intention of making it easy for him to arrange one.

James remained in the parlor for a while, feeling thoroughly befuddled by the girl. One moment she had been sharing her early life and the next sounding as though she were giving him a warning. Her behavior puzzled him greatly. Yet it made him all the more determined to understand what drove her thoughts. As he made his way to bed at last, he looked forward to the morning, when he might attempt to make sense of the unpredictable Miss Summers.

The servants brought in breakfast just before ten o'clock. As was their habit, Lydia and Papa dined in their rooms. It was the perfect time for Lydia to enlist the aid of the household staff in her effort to keep abreast of the whereabouts of Mr. Summers. Lydia waited until her maid, Sarah, drew open the curtains to display a glorious day before she said, "I shall entrust you with a task. It is very important—do you understand?"

Sarah turned wide eyes upon her mistress. Looking a bit wary, she replied, "Yes, miss?"

"I would like for all of you to keep an eye on our guest, Mr. Summers. Make it a point to know where he is at all times. Can you do that for me?"

Sarah bit her lower lip. "Of course, miss, if you like."

Lydia settled her tray comfortably upon her lap. "Then I shall take you into my confidence."

Sarah nodded, eagerness replacing her reserve.

Lydia whispered in conspiracy. "I have reason to believe that Mr. Summers wishes to harm Papa. I want all of you to tell me if you see or hear anything suspicious, as well as reporting his whereabouts."

Sarah's hazel eyes filled with excitement. "I shall keep all in secret except for those who must know. You will see, miss. He shall not make a move without having us know about it."

Lydia smiled at the girl. "I knew that I could count on you." She thought about the butler. "If Tibbs has any questions regarding my wishes, tell him to speak to me in private."

"Yes, miss. Shall you be needing me now?"

"No. You may go. Thank you, Sarah."

Sarah nodded and departed, bent upon her mission.

Lydia felt more comfortable knowing she would not be the only one watching Mr. Summers. If the servants noted anything suspicious, they would inform her, and between the lot of them she would manage to keep Papa safe.

She pulled her bedcovers close about her as she finished the light breakfast. A glance out the window told her that the rain had ceased, leaving a washed-

out, faded sky. And yet she could hear the wind rattling at the panes and knew that the morning air would
carry a chill.

After finishing with her tray, she could no longer
put off arising. So she slid her bare feet from the
cover and shivered as she donned her slippers. Sarah
fetched her riding habit and helped her disrobe and
don the heavy blue velvet that provided welcome
warmth. She pulled her hair back with pearl bar-
rettes, allowing it to fall in loose dark waves upon the
fine white lawn of her collar.

Dismissing Sarah back to her chores, she appraised
herself in the full-length mirror. The pale winter sun
had stolen the color from her cheeks. She pinched
them in an effort to restore a rosy glow. Then her hand
froze as she was struck by the pains she was taking.
She should not care what Mr. James Summers thought
of her. His good opinion meant nothing to her.

She flounced from the mirror and rummaged in
her bureau for her white gauntlet gloves that she
had bought while in London. By the time she found
them and tossed them onto the bed, she had convinced herself that her only reason for taking pains
with her dress was that she wanted Mr. Summers to
be assured that they maintained not only the house
but themselves with more than a modicum of style.

And there was no one in better style than Lydia
outfitted in her riding dress. She assured herself
that he could find no fault with either her or Papa as

she opened her hatbox to retrieve her stylish velvet slouched riding hat that so perfectly matched her dress.

Turning back to the mirror, she allowed herself a grim smile. Mr. Summers would find it to his disadvantage if he supposed her to be too naïve and bucolic to be aware of his purpose. Feeling thus, she clutched her gloves and strode down to meet Papa and Mr. Summers.

She found them waiting for her in the parlor. In spite of her resolution, Lydia found it hard not to admire Mr. Summers' wide shoulders in his well-fitting riding coat, his muscular thighs and calves showed to his advantage by his trim cord breeches. To her dismay, she noticed that he studied her with equal interest, a slow smile spreading across his face. His eyes were the cerulean blue of deep water, lit by the golden glow of sunlight that spilled across him from the open-curtained window, making him look like a chiseled form of male perfection. She wondered what he was thinking yet hoped that he had no clue as to her disturbing reaction to him. Could he tell that her pulse began to race as soon as their eyes met? She distinctly hoped that he could not. For it could easily become a fatal error if she allowed his charm to overcome her suspicion.

She averted her gaze and asked, "Are you well this morning, Papa?"

She had noticed that he looked a bit drawn and pale, as though he had not slept well. Instead of displaying his usual rigid posture, he slumped, and dark circles lay under his eyes.

"I am fine, my dear, though I might say you are fine and fair today."

Lydia flushed under the compliment. "Thank you, Papa."

Had her father noticed that she had taken extra care with her appearance? She could not bear for Papa to guess that she found Mr. Summers attractive. Not after she had promised to keep her distance from the man.

Mr. Summers bowed. "I cannot tell you how delighted I am to take this turn about the estate with two such delightful companions. And the weather was splendid to accommodate us, do you not think so, Miss Summers?"

Lydia fastened her attention upon a chubby cloud and said, "It is perfectly favorable for a ride, Mr. Summers. And I believe that we should be off. One never knows when it may turn foul again this time of year."

Mr. Summers nodded. His bright hair glistened in the sunlight. "Excellent idea. If you will lead the way to the stables, I shall be happy to follow."

He clutched his crop as he followed Lydia and Mr. Summers out the parlor doors and onto the marbled portico whose pillars rose to support the balcony on the upper floor.

They followed the cobbled path that led from the portico. The stones led one way to enter the hedged garden; the other took a path along a small brook and led to the stables. James caught the scent of the horses and felt his spirits soar. Nothing made him more relaxed than to sit perched upon a fine mount, knowing he might go wherever he liked as fast as he pleased.

They entered the stable and breathed deeply of the horses and hay, leather and grains. Obviously he and his cousin, Lydia, shared a love of the country and the enjoyment of a stimulating ride.

The stable boy hurried over. He was a short, round-faced lad with a limp in his right leg. Lydia had become fond of him since the hostler had hired him. He was always cheerful and, more important, took particular care with the horses.

He saddled her little mare, Papa's big roan, and a spirited bay for Mr. Summers. When they were all mounted, they walked the horses from the stable and headed north, where the bulk of the tenant property lay.

James could not keep his eyes from straying to Lydia. The trim lines of her jacket showed her petite

form to advantage, and her blue velvet hat looked
fine perched atop her dark hair, which fell in soft
waves across her shoulders. And yet it was more than
her appearance that intrigued James. Every time he
spoke to Lydia, he became more intrigued by her
outspoken manner coupled by her seeming reluc-
tance to warm to him. Surely she was not still angry
about the mishap with the coach.

He had imagined that he had seen a softening of
her expression when they were in the parlor. It had
passed quickly, replaced by a veil of distrust. Yet
from that brief moment he found encouragement. He
had never been a man to turn down a challenge, and
now he was determined to discover the woman who
lay behind the veil.

He brought himself back to the present as he realized that her papa was speaking to him. He reined in
to keep pace with the gentleman, reluctantly retract-
ing his gaze from Miss Summers, who rode ahead.

"Pardon me, sir?"

The older man nodded toward a thatched-roof cottage and said, "We have always prided ourselves on
our fairness to and consideration of our tenants—
have always felt it our obligation. When there is dis-
ease or misfortune, we do what we can to help out."

James nodded. He forced his bay to amble beside
the big roan.

"That is admirable, sir. You are surely an excellent
landlord."

The older man shifted to view his nephew. "I could never rest easily in my grave if I felt this estate and our tenants were being neglected or mistreated."

James felt his jaw slack with surprise. Why such suspicion of his character from both father and daughter? Had his own father been such a scamp as to engender distrust of the son?

"I assure you that I am neither negligent nor unfeeling. Though I am in no hurry to assume my post here, I will, in all good conscience, endeavor to manage the estate and the tenants in the very same excellent manner you have done."

Though less than cheerful in countenance, the elder Mr. Summers nodded and said, "On that point, you have eased my mind. Now I hope only that I shall live long enough to see my Lydia happily settled on a comfortable estate, or perhaps married to a nobleman in London."

James could not say that he shared that wish. He could think of nothing he would welcome less at this moment than to be informed of Lydia's engagement. Seeing that it would be improper to admit such sentiment to her father, he said, "I heartily understand your concern, sir. And let me further assure you that, should your early demise cause Miss Summers to have a need of residence before she is married, I would be happy to remain at my rented quarters while she resides awhile in her home."

"That is kind, indeed. You have eased my fears. I

see much of my brother in you. He was a scamp at times, but he had a heart. I never saw him be cruel to either man or animal."

"He was a good man. I was heartily sorry to lose him."

"I am glad to hear it. There should be mourning over the death of one's kin. I cannot say that has always been true of this family."

James leaned toward his uncle. "What do you mean?"

"Legend has it that your great-aunt was cheated out of her home when her husband was murdered by his own brother. Worse, in her mind, was that she had only a daughter and no son to inherit the estate."

James felt as though a dark cloud had enclosed them. "That is terrible, indeed. Surely it is not true. I cannot imagine that any man would stoop to the murder of his own brother."

The elder Mr. Summers gave a mirthless chuckle. "I fear it has happened more often than you would like to imagine—since the first brothers, Cain and Abel."

"But you called it a legend. So you are not sure it is true."

"No one ever proved it. Yet it has persisted as a murky ghost, tempting and threatening revenge with each new generation."

He turned to face James squarely. "I do not fear death. Since my wife was killed, I have had only

Lydia to keep me from longing for release from this sorrowful world. But even for my own hastened escape, I would not wish the stain of murder to rest upon any of my kin."

James frowned, mulling over his words. When he could not decipher them, he asked, "Do you feel you might be a target for revenge, Uncle?"

The older man shook his head. "Probably not. My head feels foggy today, and I fear that I am rambling. Please forgive me."

James felt foggy of brain as well. Yet he hastened to assure the elder Summers, "There is nothing to forgive. I only wish that I could understand more of what you have disclosed."

Before his uncle could reply, Lydia dropped back to join them. She cast a concerned look at her father and said, "It is cold, and you are still looking pale. I fear we have gone too far. Mr. Summers may see more of the grounds later if he likes. I believe we should go back."

Lydia was surprised when Papa did not argue but turned his horse to follow her lead. The threesome loped back to the house, the wind stinging their noses and brightening their cheeks. Pale clouds swirled above them like ghost riders waiting to swoop in pursuit.

Lydia was relieved when they reached the stable without enduring the discomfort of rain or sleet. She left the horses in the care of the stable boy and accompanied the men along the cobbled path, past the hedges, and through the French doors that led to the warmth of the downstairs parlor.

A massive log sizzled on the grate, giving both comfort and cheer to the room. Lydia urged her papa to take a chair beside the fire. "I shall ring for tea. That will warm us nicely."

She was aware that Mr. Summers studied her as she rang for the tea and gave her orders to Sarah. She shrugged off his gaze, pretending to be unaware of any interest he might take in her.

When she was seated on the settee that lay between the two chairs, she asked Mr. Summers, "Did you enjoy your ride?"

"Indeed. It was invigorating and informative as well. Your family has cared for the grounds and tenant property in a manner that should bring you pride. I hope to do as well one day. In fact, I have assured your father that I shall make it my goal to try."

"So you are well pleased with our estate. Tell me, Mr. Summers, are you a patient man?"

James frowned, clearly puzzled by her question. "I like to think that I am, when called to be so. Why do you ask?"

"Mere curiosity. I am curious about your character."

"And have you made it out yet?"

"Not entirely, I'm afraid."

James' slow, engaging smile shook Lydia's resolve.

"Then I shall endeavor to see that you come to know me better. For I do not want you to want for anything on my account."

"You are very kind, I am sure."

"It is not only kindness, my dear cousin. You see, I am as curious about you as you are about me. As you inspect my character, I feel I might get to know yours as well."

Lydia met his gaze. "I am an open book, Mr. Summers. I care about those I love, and I will do all that I can to protect them."

"That is admirable, indeed. May I ask who you are protecting and from what?"

"I am not entirely sure."

The tea arrived, interrupting their conversation.

Papa began a discourse regarding improvements to the house and grounds that had been made over the years, making Lydia wonder if he had paid any attention to the previous conversation. She poured the tea and listened while Mr. Summers asked questions about dates and workmanship, tenant taxes and grain production.

When they finished tea, Papa rose, saying, "Now I must attend to my books. Would you like to join me in the library, Mr. Summers?"

"Thank you, no. I must go to town. I have an urgent matter that requires my attention."

Lydia studied his countenance for any sign that

this trip to town had anything to do with harming Papa. Either he was accomplished at playing innocent or truly had nothing to hide, for he gave away nothing. Nonetheless, she would send one of the servants to tail him and report back regarding his activities.

When they parted company, Lydia summoned the stable boy, feeling he would be best suited to draw little attention to himself. She explained what she wanted and was pleased with the pleasure he took in doing her bidding.

"Remember, you must not be seen. Simply follow Mr. Summers, and tell me where he goes and who he sees. Do you understand?"

"Yes, miss. He shan't ever know I was watching."

Lydia pressed a coin into his hand. "You are a good boy. Now, do not lose him."

"No, miss. And I will keep out of sight."

The boy left to watch for Mr. Summers' departure. Lydia hoped his trip to town would shed some light on the reason he had arrived here. If not, the use of the servants as spies had given Lydia another idea.

She sat down at her writing desk and began to pen a letter for Mr. Summers. She frowned in concentration as she attempted to write in an unskilled and ungrammatical hand. It was imperative that he believe the letter had come from one of the servants.

When she finished, she allowed the ink to dry before folding the paper into a slightly crooked square.

She would place the note under James' door while he was out. And when he returned, she hoped his reaction would tell her all that she needed to know. If he fell into her trap, she would inform the constable. At the least, he would be sent away forthwith. And if he ever dared to enter Derbyshire again before her father died, she would see that he was arrested.

She walked with determination to Mr. Summers' chambers and slipped the note under his door. Now all she need do was to wait . . . wait and be ready to pounce when he fell into her trap.

She settled in the downstairs drawing room and glanced at the round clock above the mantel. In three hours or so she would know the truth. In three hours or so he would have read the note and been driven by greed and curiosity to reveal his motive.

Chapter Four

James returned late in the afternoon, having posted his letter and then whiled away a pleasant hour in the pub. The last thing upon his mind was that of finding a letter slipped beneath his door and addressed to him in an untidy script. He opened it and felt his jaw drop open as he scanned the ill-written lines.

He shook his head and wondered why anyone would put forth such a horrid proposal. It was beyond belief. With one thought in his mind, he spun on his heel, clutching the letter in his hand. His host must be warned, and Lydia as well.

He hurried down to search them out. He found Lydia in the parlor. For once he was not distracted by her beauty.

"Where is your father? I must speak to him at once."

She arched a delicate eyebrow. "He is resting. Perhaps I might assist you."

"Upon arriving back, I had a most unpleasant shock. Nothing I experienced in war prepared me for this outrageous proposition."

Lydia glanced at the paper in his hand and felt a guilty flush stain her cheeks. To cover her discomfiture, she said, "Indeed, you look very vexed. May I ask what has disturbed you?"

"This letter. Did you know that you have a servant who wishes to profit from your father's death?"

Lydia swallowed hard. "What makes you think that is so?"

James thrust the letter toward Lydia. "Read this, and you will see."

Lydia unfolded the rumpled note and pretended to read it carefully, knowing full well what it said. While she had hoped he would prove his innocence, she had not expected to feel like such a villain for concocting the scheme. And yet, how else was she to know if he would have been enticed to meet with the fabricated servant behind the hollyhock hedge? And now that he was here in the parlor casting her ploy back into her lap, she wondered what she should do.

She looked up at him, meeting his clear blue eyes, and decided to stall for time. "This is disturbing. I have been worried that something like this would happen."

"Then you see why we must warn your papa. And I must go at once and confront the scoundrel who penned this note. We shall have him arrested forthwith so that he will never threaten anyone again."

His agitation was obvious as he paced the parlor. Lydia decided that he must surely be innocent of any desire to hasten his inheritance. If not, he was putting on quite a show to win her confidence. Could it be that he had disclosed the letter because he did not trust the servant? Yet even as she tried to convince herself of the possibility of his guilt, her heart told her that his distress was genuine. For it would take fine acting skills indeed to simulate either the urgency that he displayed or the indignation sketched upon his face.

Lydia bit her lip, feeling even more discomposed. "I shall speak to Papa as soon as he awakens. Perhaps you had best go to the hedge and catch the scoundrel."

James nodded and turned on his heel, leaving the note with Lydia.

She scowled at the paper before tearing it into shreds and throwing it into the fire. Then, sinking back into her chair, she muttered, "Now what have I done? As usual, I have acted without thinking."

Surely when Mr. Summers failed to find the servant, he would calm himself and decide that Papa was not in danger.

Nonetheless, she would have to admit her ruse to Papa. As she was sure he would not approve, she decided to put off telling him until just before supper. If she was lucky, she might convince him to play along and hide the truth from Mr. Summers. And when Mr. Summers was gone from their house, it would no longer matter.

She glanced up to see the maid appear.

"You have a visitor, miss. Shall I show him in?"

Lydia nodded, wondering who it might be.

James trod softly along the path to the hollyhock hedges. He scanned the grounds as he loitered near the bushes, expecting at any moment to have the servant pop out. After some time had passed, he peered into the hedges, checked the path, and frowned. Surely he had not scared the villain away, for it was obvious that he had come alone. He crossed his arms over his gray overcoat and breathed steam into the frosty air as he scanned the windows of the house. Perhaps someone was watching him, debating whether to come forward.

Another quarter hour passed in which he saw no one. Finally he turned and headed back to the house. No doubt the servant had lost his nerve. James wished he had come forward, for it was a terrible risk to have someone so disloyal in the house. He decided that he would make every effort to discover the author of the note and see that he or she was summarily dismissed.

He ignored the bite of the brisk wind. He could think only of how much this must have upset Lydia. Though she had not gone to hysterics over the note, she must be suffering terrible distress. After hearing her father confess the murderous history of the family, he understood the burden of apprehension that she bore in her heart.

A growing sense of protection toward both his fair cousin and his uncle enveloped him as he strode back to the French doors that led into the parlor. For as much as it rested within his power, he would see that no harm came to either of them. For he could not stand the thought of his vibrant cousin clad in black mourning, her flashing dark eyes dulled by grief. It was not to be borne. He would speak to her, and together they would devise a means to protect his uncle. If she liked, he would remain indefinitely at the estate to provide a degree of protection to the older man.

The thought pleased him. He could be of use to his cousin as well as get to know her better. None of the sisters or daughters of the men he knew in India were nearly as pretty or lively as this English rose.

Inspired by his plan, he resolved to tell her at once what he had decided.

Lydia cringed when James strode into the parlor. He was far more intriguing than her present guest, and she had no desire for him to think that she had an attachment to Reginald. If it were within her power, she would make Reginald vanish. His arrival had interrupted her thoughts regarding the best way to explain to Papa the awkward situation she had created.

Yet, like it or not, Reginald had swept into the room, bestowing a tight smile. She had no choice save to ask him to sit while she clutched her lace kerchief and hoped his visit would prove short.

After a bit of small talk he said, "My sister tells me that your cousin is to arrive any day."

"He has already arrived. He came yesterday, in fact."

"And are his manners pleasing? I hear he has served aboard ship for the last few years."

"Indeed, he is quite civil and considerate."

"I am glad to hear it. One would not want to be turned from one's home by a man who was less than charming."

Lydia felt her ire rise. "I am sure he has no intention of turning anyone out in the near future."

Reginald raised a pale eyebrow. "One can never be sure when property is at stake. It does surprising things to people."

Lydia stiffened. "I am sure that is true. And I thank you for the warning. However, I have already thought of that danger, and I am convinced that Mr. Summers is not the sort of man to force circumstances to his will."

Reginald snorted. "I should like to meet this chap who has won your confidence so completely, so that I might admire him as well."

"I am not a simpleton. Nor did I say that I admire him," Lydia protested.

Reginald's pale eyes glittered, baiting her with a narrowed gaze. "You must forgive me. I find your praise of another man hard to bear."

"I call things as I see them."

Lydia was tired of the banter and wished he would leave. She was on the verge of inventing a headache when James popped into the room.

The men stared candidly at one another in a manner that challenged the right of the other to be there. At last Lydia broke the silence by saying, "This is Mr. Reginald Smyth. He was just saying that he wished to meet you, Mr. Summers."

Reginald stood and bowed. The two men were very nearly the same height, both blue-eyed and fair. Yet while Reginald seemed as somber and pasty-faced as a recluse, James had the color and vibrancy of one who embraced life.

James bowed in return. "Are you a friend of Miss Summers?"

"A neighbor and a friend," Reginald replied.

His tone gave such a hint of suggestion. Lydia hastened to add, "Mr. Smyth's sister, Eve, and I are friends. I met Reginald as a consequence of our friendship."

James nodded. "I see."

He did not feel free to speak to Lydia in front of her long-faced guest. If the man would only take his leave, they might begin plans to ensure her father's health. As it stood, he could only accept Lydia's invitation to join them and bide his time.

He fidgeted impatiently with his cuff, knowing that Lydia must be eager to discover if the servant had joined him. Not wishing to lengthen Mr. Smyth's visit, he took part in the conversation only when the necessity of being polite forced him to do so. All the while he wondered if Lydia cared for Mr. Smyth. He hoped she did not, for he found the man entirely tedious and dull.

At long last Reginald drew a regretful sigh and said, "I must be getting back. Eve is expecting me and will be impatient for news of you both. She is a great admirer of Miss Lydia and will, no doubt, think well of you also, Mr. Summers. You must meet soon."

"Perhaps we shall." James nodded, wishing only that Mr. Smyth would be off.

Reginald stood, and the others rose with him.

"Perhaps I might bring Eve for a visit later in the week, if that is convenient." His gaze fell expectantly upon Lydia.

If she could have thought of any excuse, she would have used it. However, as she was at a loss as to how to keep them from coming, she said, "That would be delightful. In the meantime, please give Eve my regards."

He bowed deeply and said, "I should be glad to do so."

After he left, she sought a quick escape from having to face James. She sidled toward the doorway and said, "I should be going up to check on Papa. I thought he looked a bit peaked this morning."

James was instantly beside her. He took her elbow and drew her back to the settee. Settling beside her, he said, "Do you not wish to know what happened in the garden?"

She cocked her head and feigned interest. "But of course. You were to meet a servant."

James nodded, his eyes bright with fervor. "He never showed up. What do you make of that? No doubt he lost his nerve. But how is he to be discovered now?"

Lydia swallowed hard. She was only too aware of his knee resting warmly against her leg, the intense blue of his eyes and the straight line of his nose. How would she ever tell him the truth? He would surely be furious with her for putting him to her test.

She decided to save the truth for another time. After all, she had not concocted the note to benefit herself. It was all in the interest of protecting her father. Perhaps in time James would come to understand.

She spoke slowly, choosing her words. "I am very sorry no one came forward, for I had hoped to learn his identity. For now, I shall have to be content with keeping a watchful eye upon Papa."

James nodded. A lock of blond hair fell onto his forehead. He brushed it back impatiently. "In that endeavor I am determined to offer my assistance. I shall remain as long as you like, armed and ready for any need that may arise."

Lydia dropped her gaze. She felt her cheeks flush with shame to hear his dedication to this false alarm. With every word he uttered, she became more convinced of the sincerity of his profession and more persuaded that she had been hasty in assuming that he had come in malice.

She forced a smile. "You are very kind. I am sure whoever wrote the note will not act without your assistance. And since you are not interested in the proposition, we have nothing to fear."

James considered her words. "Nonetheless, I shall remain alert."

Lydia nodded. "Thank you. Now I truly must run up and check on Papa."

"Of course. Be sure to caution him of the danger."

"Indeed. I shall tell him all that has transpired."

Lydia exited, bearing her guilty conscience. She would confess all to Papa and pray that he would guard her confidence. Then, when Mr. Summers went away, she could forget all about this debacle. A small pang of doubt stabbed her heart. How easy would it be to forget the look of concern in his cerulean blue eyes, his congenial manner, or the wavy blond hair that fell upon his forehead, tempting her to curl it upon her finger?

She shook free these thoughts as she climbed the stairs. If confession was good for the soul, she was about to improve her health. She only hoped she felt better when she had done so.

She knocked on Papa's door, expecting him to bid her enter. By this time of day he was usually at his writing desk, penning out his accounts. She was surprised to receive no answer. Had he gone out? Surely not. The weather was frightfully cold, and she could not remember that he had mentioned any errands.

She knocked again and heard her effort rewarded by a groan. Her heart leaped to her throat. Perhaps he had fallen, hit his head, or broken a bone. She shoved open the door and entered.

She blinked in the darkened room. Papa had not lit a candle. And, having just left the light of a dozen candles nestling in their sconces in the hall, she could make out very little in the dimness.

"Papa?"

The shuffle of bedding and another groan led her to his bedside. She could just make out the outline of his long-limbed body resting beneath the blankets. She knelt beside him and rubbed his cheek. Her gentle touch stirred him. In a raspy voice he said, "Lydia. I fear that I am unwell. Could you get me some water?"

"Certainly."

She groped along the bedside table until she found a candle. She took it to the hall and used a lit candle to set it alight. Then, returning to the bedchamber, she set the candle on the table beside the bed.

It was unusual for Papa to be unwell and even more uncommon for him to take to his bed. Her worry spun out of control. What if his illness proved serious?

All the while that she poured his water from the ceramic pitcher on the washstand into a glass, her mind whirled with fearful thoughts. The only comfort she achieved was in knowing that Mr. Summers was in the parlor below, ready to assist if she needed him. He would go for the doctor if she asked him to do so. She felt as confident of it as she did of her own name. After all, had he not just pledged to stay as long as she desired his presence? Now, with Papa sick, she found his words of more comfort than she liked to admit.

She sat with Papa as he dozed. Even in the pale candlelight she could see that his face was flushed with fever. He shook with chills under the heavy bedding and complained of an aching in his bones.

She managed to get him to take only a little more water. Perhaps soup would be better. She summoned Sarah and said, "Papa is ill. Go down to the kitchen and have Cook make him some warm broth."

Sarah nodded. "Shall I feed him, miss?"

"No, I think I had better stay."

Papa squeezed her hand and said, "We have a guest. You must go down to supper and make my apologies. I will be fine here with Sarah."

She hesitated. "I do not wish to leave you so ill."

"It is only for a short while, and Sarah will fetch you if you are needed, will you not, girl?"

"Yes, sir."

Lydia, not wanting to agitate him, finally agreed. Yet she pulled Sarah aside and said, "You must tell me immediately if he gets worse."

"Yes, miss, I will."

Her brow puckered and small face clouded with worry, she left the room soundlessly to carry out the wish of her mistress. And Lydia was grateful that she could trust her to do exactly as requested.

When Sarah returned, she carried a bowl of warm broth covered with a dish towel. Lydia moved aside and allowed Sarah to take the chair beside the bed. Reluctantly she turned for the door.

"Remember. Come and tell me if he gets worse."

Sarah uncovered the broth. "Try not to worry, miss. Cook says chicken broth will have him up in no time."

Lydia smiled. "Thank you, Sarah. For now I shall trust him to you."

Alone in her own chamber, Lydia perused her wardrobe. She finally chose a navy crinoline with a scooped neckline and long, fitted sleeves that ended with ivory lace. She slipped into the dress and piled her hair atop her head before adding a pearl necklace that had belonged to her mother. She fingered the pearls, so beautiful yet hard and cold.

Her mother had been wearing them on the night she was murdered. She hesitated, fingering the beads as a shiver crept down her spine. Silly, she thought, for something as harmless as a set of pearls to make her think of murder.

She latched them about her neck, determined not to let herself be overtaken by the emotions of a childhood loss. She turned from the full-length oval mirror and pulled on her creamy satin slippers. She would be good company to James tonight. She owed it to him after the lie she had concocted that afternoon.

The only good thing about Papa's illness was that James was unlikely to learn the truth. There would be plenty of time when Papa got well to urge him to cooperate with her fabrication and play the part of an anxious heir.

She paused in the hallway and took a deep breath to calm her frazzled nerves. Not only did she have Papa to worry over, but her feelings for James had taken a disconcerting turn. She had not wished to find him attractive, had planned to thoroughly dislike him. And yet, two days after meeting him, she found it impossible for her heart to carry out these intentions. Nonetheless, she knew she must be cautious. It was too soon for an understanding between them. And he had not given her reason to believe that he had any serious intentions toward her. His admiring looks could easily be mere flirting, his desire to protect them, merely a kind heart. And for those reasons, she must guard her own heart and keep from risking it if it were only to be broken.

She descended the stairs, still trying to sort her mix of emotions. James was already in the parlor, awaiting her arrival. He held a glass of brandy in his long, tapered fingers, swirling the liquid thoughtfully until he noticed Lydia sweeping into the room.

Lydia's presence had the same intoxicating effect as James' brandy. Everything about her intrigued him—her large dark eyes, her wine red lips, the vibrancy that emanated from every inch of her small form, and her candor, which left no doubt of her opinions.

He knew he was staring. Yet how could he help but stare? She was exquisite in her elegant blue dress. Her dark hair, which was clasped atop her head, showed her slender neck, outlined with pearls, to perfection. The tendrils that fell in soft curls behind her head tempted him to reach out a finger and draw them to his lips.

Drawing upon his reserve of self-discipline, he bowed instead. "You look lovely tonight."

"Thank you. I am sorry to be late. Papa is unwell. I believe he has a touch of the ague. I have left him in the care of my maid."

James raised a brow. "Your maid? Are you sure she can be trusted? Perhaps she penned the note that I received."

Lydia shook her head. "Not Sarah. I trust her completely. However, I hope you will not take offense if I do not linger after supper. I am anxious about my father and wish to check on him."

"No, indeed. I am sorry to hear that he is unwell. Is there anything that I may do?"

Lydia smiled, and he felt as though the sun had appeared through a haze of clouds.

She looked into his eyes, and he felt as though he were drowning in the depths of a dark chocolate pool.

"You are kind. There is nothing to be done at present but to see to his comfort. Should he grow worse by morning, we shall have need of the doctor."

"I would be happy to be of service should the need arise."

Lydia tilted her head, studying James from her diminutive height. "You are a most obliging gentleman—not at all what I expected."

James laughed. "What did you expect?"

Lydia flushed a crimson red. "I am sorry. I should not have said that."

"On the contrary. I find your honesty refreshing. I cannot abide ladies who refuse to speak their minds.

Lydia caught her lip between her teeth. She was too outspoken. At school she had occasionally offended teachers or friends with her opinions. She had thought to conquer the habit. Yet she found that she had come no closer to mastering her tongue now than then. Only now she had more to lose. She must master herself when she was around James, become less transparent. He might admire ladies who spoke their minds, but it could be to her disadvantage to do so.

She felt his eyes upon her as he changed the subject.

"There is a beautiful snowfall outside. Would you care to take a look?"

Lydia nodded.

He extinguished the candles before leading her to the window. He pulled back the heavy drapery, and Lydia caught her breath. White flakes drifted down softly from a black velvet sky, sticking to tree limbs and covering the ground in a fine powder.

They stood close, so near that Lydia caught the fresh scent of his clean shirt. Her pulse gave a lurch as she felt herself drawn to him with feelings that she had never experienced with any other man, certainly not Reginald, whose stiff efforts to court her had left her unmoved. She could never be tempted by a man whose hands promised to be as cold as his eyes. Only a man of deep passion and strong character could ever win her respect and love.

James broke into her reverie as he whispered, "It has been so long since I have seen snow. After living in India for so many years, I had forgotten how beautiful the trees and grounds look cloaked in a white blanket."

Lydia nodded. "I love to look across the fields when nothing has touched them and they are pure and white."

He looked down at her and said, "Indeed. Nothing could be so beautiful."

"Perhaps if Papa is better tomorrow, I might walk about the grounds."

"If you could bear my company, I should like to go with you."

Her mind warned her, yet her heart urged her to reply, "I should like company. I take most of my walks alone, as Papa does not fancy getting out."

"Well, I fancy a walk most any time. Every season has its pleasures and beauty, much like the course of our lives."

"I have never thought of it that way, but I suppose you are right."

"Indeed, if we fail to appreciate one season of life, it flees and is gone forever. However, I am convinced that if we try, we can find meaning and beauty in each stage of our existence."

She looked up at him, admiring his wisdom, and wished she could make out his features, which were hidden by the inky darkness of the room.

"I suppose I have much to learn," she said.

He brushed a finger across her cheek. "And much time to learn it."

Lydia shivered at his touch and felt remorse at her earlier deceit. Would he find her appealing if he knew how she had distrusted him, lied to him, and tested him? Not wanting to face her conscience in this tender moment, she stepped away. "We must be getting to supper. The food will grow cold, and I must not tarry too long before I check on Papa."

James dropped his hand to his side. "Of course. We shall go at once."

As he followed Lydia from the room, James chastised himself for his impetuous action. His lack of restraint would be his undoing one day. And now he had been too bold, too quick to reveal his affection and had, no doubt, given offense. From now on he would be more careful, more reserved. For the last thing he wanted to do was to drive Lydia away from him. He would hold his affections in check and hope that, one day soon, Lydia would welcome them.

Chapter Five

The mood of intimacy diminished as they left the dark cloister of the parlor and entered the candlelit dining room. The rich luster of the cherrywood table and the bright white china and sparkling silver gave cheer to the room. The aroma of roasted pork and gravy, potatoes and onions were a powerful reminder to Lydia that she had not eaten in hours. And yet, if she dared, she would trade all of it for a few brief moments in James' arms.

She shook the thought from her head. She should be thankful instead that the harvest had been plentiful and their share of the tenants' crops had filled the pantries to overflowing, proof that the fields of Holly Green Manor were valuable property. Mr. Summers would find life comfortable here, should he prove to be a good manager of the estate.

The thought of having him own the house did not incense her as it had at first. Instead, it filled her with dismay that, at some future time, she would part with James as well as the estate. And the idea of another woman, both as mistress of Holly Green Manor and wife of James, was not a pleasant thought.

She glanced up to see him watching her. He was seated just across the table, making it difficult to look up without meeting his eyes. And though he did not accuse her, she knew from his subtle shift in mood that her swift removal from the parlor had sobered his display of affection. Her heart ached with the uncertainty of what he might be thinking of her. Did he think her cold and proud, too good for a seaman?

She wished Papa were there. Though he was of a taciturn nature, his presence would have offered a buffer from the forced intimacy. But he was not here, and she would have to get through the evening as gracefully as possible while keeping her heart intact.

She spooned a bite of creamy potato, yellowed by butter, into her mouth and swallowed without tasting. She forced herself to smile up at James and say, "I should like to hear more about your adventures in India. Several of my friends at school lived there as children."

He returned her smile. "I should not say that I had many 'adventures,' except for the ones created by my naughtiness as a child. I preferred the native children over many of those from England. I was forever running off to play, worrying my nanny and getting into scrapes."

"Was it beautiful there?"

He nodded. "It was. It rained a great deal, making both gardens and countryside verdant and always blooming with colorful flowers. I often roamed the hills, even in the rain, looking for mongeese. But it was most often a warm rain. I was lucky not to have been bitten by a cobra, though I backed away from one, none too soon, on one occasion."

Lydia shivered. "I should hate to worry about snakes when I walked."

"That is why I believe even a snowy walk here to be preferable to my childhood walks there."

Lydia nodded. "You will still come walking with me tomorrow if Papa is improved, will you not?" She held her breath, lest he say he had changed his mind.

"I will come. Fresh air is good for the constitution."

She felt relieved to see a teasing light in his eyes.

They finished their meal, and James ordered his coffee to be taken in the parlor. Lydia smiled regretfully and said, "I hope you will excuse me. I must see to Papa."

"Of course. I shall be anxious to hear how he is doing. Please feel free to call on me, day or night, if I may be of assistance."

"I shall, though I hope there will be no need."

Her brow creased with worry as she climbed the stairs to go to her papa's chamber. She hoped to find him improved and resting well. It was hard to bear his illness at the same time that she was worried about his safety from outside harm. But surely he was better. *He must be better*, she told herself, as she opened his door.

Sarah sat beside the bed, just where Lydia had left her. Instead of a bowl of soup, she held a cool cloth in one hand and laid it upon Papa's head.

"He is very hot, miss, and still complains of aches in his bones."

Lydia caught her lip. "Thank you, Sarah. I shall take over now. You go and have your supper."

The girl nodded and slipped from the room.

Lydia managed to get her father to take a few spoonfuls of soup. She sponged his head from time to time and spoke words of encouragement. Just after midnight he seemed to settle into a comfortable sleep. Lydia found her own head nodding and allowed herself the luxury of dozing in her chair.

She awoke sometime in the early gray dawn and saw that he was still sleeping peacefully. Sighing with relief, she tiptoed to her room and sank into the downy covers of her bed. She awoke a few hours later with the full brilliance of shimmering sunlight slanting across her coverlet. She shifted lazily and stretched her toes in the blissful warmth. Oh, how she disliked cold floors and chilly hallways. The tedious confinement of winter wore on her. If only it could always be summer. She would dress lightly and spend her days out of doors, riding and picking wildflowers and visiting the tenants.

She sat up and pulled on her cashmere peignoir. With the self-discipline of years of early rising while at school, she swung her feet to the floor and into her slippers. She had not bothered to braid her hair, and it fell in a wild, tumbling cascade down her back. She gave it a few brisk brush strokes before scurrying down the hall to check on Papa.

He opened bleary eyes when she entered the room to sit beside him. She took his hand and asked, "How are you feeling?"

He nodded. "Better, I believe. I do not ache so much anymore."

"Are you hungry?"

"A little, perhaps."

"I shall tell Sarah to bring up some toast and soft eggs. And you must have some tea. You are still dreadfully pale."

Geoffrey patted her hand and said, "You worry over me too much. I shall be fine. Surely you have something with which to amuse yourself this morning."

Lydia pulled aside a window curtain and gazed outside. The leaden sky looked as though it might overflow at any moment and spill its load of snow.

She glanced back at Papa and said, "Mr. Summers did ask to join me on a walk."

Geoffrey attempted to push himself up on his pillow and then gave up the weak attempt. A deep frown creased his forehead. "I do not want you taking up with Mr. Summers. I grant that he is an amiable chap. But he is also heir to the estate. If he should be in danger, so would you."

Lydia gave a nervous laugh. "It is only a walk, Papa. And we have not had even the hint of a threat since he arrived."

Geoffrey sighed. "That is true. Still, you must promise me not to get attached. I do not want to see you either endangered or an early widow."

"La, Papa. That is not going to happen."

"Then you must run along and have a good time." Looking exhausted from the conversation, Geoffrey closed his eyes. Lydia decided to wait until later in the day to mention the test to which she had put James. Papa would not be up and about today anyway and was unlikely to converse with him.

She sat with him a bit longer, feeling uncertain about leaving for her walk. His lips were pallid, his face even more thin. Perhaps he needed nourishment to build up his strength.

When he roused, she rose and rang for the maid. "I shall have Sarah see to your breakfast, and you must promise to eat it."

Geoffrey gave a weak wave of his hand that she

hoped was agreement. "Go and take your walk. I shall be fine."

She smiled. "I shall be back soon to check on you."

She left at last, closing the door softly behind her. She found Sarah in the hallway and gave her orders. Then she slipped into her own room to dress warmly in a gown of navy velvet. She pulled on her warmest wool stockings and took her lined, satin cape from the peg in the wardrobe. Then she scuttled downstairs to inquire as to the whereabouts of Mr. Summers. When the butler informed her that James was in the library, she could hardly contain her anticipation while she ate the food spread before her in the sunny breakfast room.

She lingered in front of the library door, suddenly bashful about making her entrance. She brought her hand to her cheek where James had touched her so gently the night before. Would he touch her again? The question brought a mixture of hope and anxiety. Did she want to fall in love with James Summers? She shivered, leaving the question unanswered as she turned the knob of the library door and stepped inside.

James sat in the upright chair beside the hearth, holding a thick volume. He looked up immediately when Lydia stepped through the doorway. An approving smile lit his face, and she flushed from head to toe with pleasurable warmth. Since she was too far from the fireplace to explain it away, she could only admit to herself that James had that effect upon her.

He set the book aside and stood. She was struck by his height as he looked down and said, "You look lovely this morning. And I see that you are holding your cloak. An outing, perhaps? I hope this means that your papa has improved."

"Indeed. And as he is better, I thought to take a turn about the garden."

"Then I shall be more than happy to join you. I shall fetch my coat at once."

He excused himself and strode down the hall to the coatrack. Curious about the book, Lydia picked up what proved to be the collected works of Lord Byron. A rush of pleasure filled her veins with the discovery that James was a poetic man. Perhaps he might read her sonnets as they sat together beside a cozy fire or under a tree when springtime warmed the earth. It would be lovely to be courted by a man whose voice spoke with passion and whose eyes flashed like the clear blue of an ocean as he recited words of love and loss.

She started and nearly dropped the volume as James trod back into the room. He grinned as he saw her hastily return the book to the table beside the chair. "Do you enjoy poetry, Miss Lydia?"

His tone was serious, yet a teasing glint shone in his eyes.

Lydia felt as though her runaway daydream

showed clearly on her face. She stammered, "Y-yes. Well, that is, I like some poetry. I do not read it often, but I believe it can be nice."

James laughed. "No, you do not strike me as the type who would sit long enough to read much of anything. Perhaps I might tempt you with a reading beside a warm fire on a particularly cold evening."

For once Lydia was at a loss for words. She felt transparent. Yet what harm could there be in accepting an invitation in her own home?

"I would enjoy that. And I assure you that I can sit perfectly still when engrossed."

A twinkle shown in his eyes. "Then I assure you, I shall keep you spellbound."

Lydia had no doubt that he was capable of holding her interest. He had already proven that fact. The question was, could he be trusted not to break her heart?

She led the way through the French doors and across the veranda to where the cobbled garden path twisted and turned between holly hedges until it reached a rectangular garden. The pruned rosebushes, pride and center of the garden, were bare and brown. A white stone bench sat at the edge of the garden, its curved legs resting gracefully upon the pebbles.

James pulled her down to sit upon the bench. He became serious as he attacked the subject of the letter. "Have you had any hints as to the author of the vile missive that I received yesterday?"

Lydia burrowed into her cloak, relieved that he could not easily see her face.

"I do not believe that it was one of the servants, for I know them all too well to believe them capable of such an act."

James nodded. "Someone from the stable, perhaps? The hostler or that boy who brought our horses?"

"I do not believe that it was either of them."

"Then who do you suppose wrote the letter?"

"Perhaps it was not one of our servants at all."

James frowned. "Someone from outside the house?"

Lydia's cheeks, hidden inside her cloak, felt aflame. How had she gotten herself into such a mess? And how would she get out? James would not drop the matter, and her conscience pricked her every time he brought it up. They could never have an honest friendship as long as this was between them. And though she had thought she could do so, she realized she could not stand to see him each day and hide behind his ignorance of the truth.

She licked her dry lips and plunged ahead before she lost her courage. "I do not know how to say this, and I am heartily ashamed of my actions. My only excuse is that I am fond of my father and determined to keep him from harm."

James frowned when she paused. "What are you trying to tell me?"

She took a deep breath. "Only that I am the one who wrote the letter. I feared that you had come with the intention of hurrying your possession of the estate. I hoped to force your hand and see if you scurried off to a secret meeting, hoping to find an accomplice."

Before he could reply, she hastened to say, "I do not suspect you any longer. It is only that, when you first arrived, I knew nothing about your character, and I knew of no other way to ascertain it."

He was thoughtful for a moment while she held her breath, wondering if this would be the end of their budding relationship. It would be awkward to have him rebuff her, for they were sure to be thrown together now and again in a village as small as theirs.

James took Lydia's hand and held it with his leather-gloved one. He pushed back her hood and looked deeply into her eyes. "If you had known me longer before you wrote the letter, I would have been vexed indeed. As it is, I can only be warmed by the protective affection you carry for your father. You are a unique little person, my dear cousin. And with every passing day, my admiration for you grows."

He wondered if he had expressed his feelings too ardently. When she had turned from him last evening, he had vowed to tread carefully. Yet now, at the first opportunity, he flung himself headlong into an effort to assure her of his devotion.

And yet as he watched her luminous dark eyes soften, he knew he had chosen the right path. To be able to express himself honestly, to be candid instead of careful, suited him much better than playing a guessing game that left them both uncertain.

She smiled up at him and said, "I am so happy that you are not angry. You see, I had convinced myself of your motives before I met you, and then, when you came, I was afraid to trust my changed feelings."

His heart pounded as he leaned closer, whispering softly, "Is there anything else I can do to assure you?"

She swallowed. He could see the rapid pulse in her throat, and he wondered if she shared the attraction that heated his veins, making him unconscious of the white flakes that drifted from the gray sky. He cast aside his resolve and claimed her mouth tentatively, sensitive to any motion she might make to draw away.

She did not withdraw but allowed him to linger upon lips that were sweet and soft as down. Her lashes fell against her creamy cheeks, fluttering slightly as his lips pressed upon her softly yielding mouth.

When he drew back to look at her, she opened her eyes, eyes that were filled with a dreamy haze. She smiled up at him and said, "I feel most certain now that you are not angry with me."

A mischievous gleam filled his eyes. A snowflake landed on her small pert nose, and he leaned down to kiss it away. In reply to her comment he said,

"Should you become the least bit uncertain as to my feelings, I should be happy to repeat my assurance."

Her laugh rang into the silent, swirling world where damp flakes clung to trees and bushes, icing them in dainty white frosting. Fresh snowfall covered the cobbles and gardens, turning their sanctuary into a fairyland for two.

Feigning shock, Lydia replied, "I do not believe that I should allow such liberties, sir. Indeed, should you try, I would have to pelt you with a handful of snow."

His blue eyes glittered. "Ah, but you would not dare, madam."

"Would I not? Perhaps you do not know me well at all."

Faster than she could react, he leaned forward and bestowed a quick kiss upon her nose. He watched in delight as her eyes widened with surprise. Then, before he could suspect her intention, she scooped a handful of snow from the end of the bench and pelted him full in the chest. With a laugh, she rose and attempted to scoop more from the pathway in front of their seat.

James was too quick and grabbed her about the waist. She wriggled and demanded release, yet he held fast. At last she turned demurely in his arms, looked up, and said, "I should like to know what will procure my freedom."

He longed to hold her captive forever, cherishing

the feel of her small warm body in his arms. And yet he knew the temperature was dropping and she would soon be chilled. He would have to release her now and hope for another excuse for such intimacy.

He gave her a mock frown and said, "The only hope for your release is a promise that no more snow shall be pelted upon my person."

She tipped her face up to him and asked with a challenging grin, "And if I do not promise?"

James was so close that Lydia could feel his breath upon her cheek. Her heart pounded with uncertainty. Would he kiss her again? Even without a kiss, Lydia could not think of any place she would rather be than trapped securely in James Summers' arms. And if he did kiss her? She felt her cheeks warm with the realization that she would raise no prim protest should he do so. She had always abhorred the coy games played by the girls at school. They toyed and teased and tried to make one suitor jealous of another. The games became so complex that she sometimes wondered if they quite lost track of their own feelings. Lydia was not one to hide her thoughts when it was much simpler to say and do exactly what she felt.

He smiled down at her and said, "Then I shall be forced to hold you prisoner."

The snow was falling harder now, sticking to their lashes and covering the top of James' hat. Yet, held close to his body, she did not feel the cold, nor mind the flakes that brushed her cheeks like a soft kiss before melting on her warm skin.

He chuckled softly. "I see that you are the intractable sort. If you will not promise, then I shall have to hope that you will behave yourself. I cannot allow you to freeze."

He kept one arm around her waist as they headed back to the warmth of the house. Lydia hoped to take tea with James beside the fire after she checked on Papa. Now that she had told James about the letter, she need not tell Papa, nor seek his cooperation. It was a profound relief to have the burden of guilt lifted from her heart. And, happily, instead of driving a wedge between them, it had brought them together.

Her thoughts were bent upon her wondrous discovery of James' feelings for her when she was suddenly jerked from her reverie by the sight of Reginald Smyth's pale face peering from the parlor door. If only it were a pleasant summer day, she would turn about and insist upon leading James upon such an extensive tour of the grounds that Reginald would be forced to leave before they returned.

She had always found him tedious company and was in no mood to have her enjoyment marred by his reproachful gaze. His pale eyes raised goose bumps on her flesh. And while Eve could be just as haughty, there was a coldness in Reginald that made her wonder if he cared for anyone, including his sister. That he would get ahead one day, she was sure. He had stated his ambitions in a way that told her he would do anything it took to raise his fortunes and propel him to the position he believed he deserved. The insufferable man. She would be forced to sit for at least an hour in his company when she wished to be alone with James.

Still, there was nothing to be done except endure. So she allowed James to escort her into the parlor, where she greeted not only Reginald, but also Eve, whose blue eyes lit with interest as Lydia and James entered the warmth of the parlor together.

Eve rose to her impressive height, leaving Lydia to feel like a waif dwarfed in a hooded cloak. She threw back her hood and forced a smile. She stepped forward and said, "How brave of you to come to visit on such a wintry day."

Reginald's tight lips lengthened into a smile. "I could not keep my sister away once she heard about a newcomer to town."

He turned his attention to James. "You must excuse her enthusiasm. It is not often that someone new arrives in our village."

James' gaze flicked over Eve. "It is my pleasure to be here. I have been made to feel completely at home."

Lydia could not forget her duty as hostess, even if she was less than enthusiastic about her guests. She spoke with as much enthusiasm as she could muster.

"Eve, I would like to present my cousin, Mr. James Summers. Mr. Summers, this is my friend, Miss Eve Smyth. You have already met Mr. Smyth."

James bowed. "It is a pleasure, miss."

Eve curtseyed. "I must admit that I have been most curious to meet you. I dared not wait for an invitation from Lydia. She is little concerned with matters of society. I do believe the dear girl would rather spend her time tramping through the snow."

Underneath the fondness in her tone, Lydia detected a criticism of her behavior. Eve made her sound like a thoughtless child, while presenting herself as a refined young woman. Wondering how this would affect James' opinion of her left her with a hollow feeling in the pit of her stomach.

She derived some comfort as James thoughtfully took her damp cape and set it, along with his coat, upon the hearth to dry. Acting out of habit, Lydia said, "Please, do sit. I shall ring for tea."

The small group settled near the fire, Eve and Reginald taking the settee while James and Lydia took the chairs on either side. "Do tell us about yourself, Mr. Summers. Lydia seemed to know very little of your background," Eve said.

As they waited for tea, James spoke of his early voyage to India, the death of his mother, and his early childhood with his father. And while Eve peppered him with questions, Reginald spoke not a word but cast an occasional glance Lydia's direction.

Tea arrived by the time James broached his recent service in the royal Navy. Eve moved to the edge of her seat, ignoring the dainty cup and small cakes set before her by the young maid. "You are brave, Mr. Summers, to have endured the hardships of India those many years."

He chuckled as he reached for his tea. "You forget, Miss Smyth, I knew nothing else. I arrived in India as a small child."

"La. I can tell that you are a man of adventure. You joined the king's Navy and proved your loyalty and courage in battle. Those are traits I admire."

"Thank you for your kind words. However, I must assure you that I served with many men more courageous than myself."

Eve raised her fair eyebrows. "And you are modest too. Is he not modest, Reginald?"

Lydia glanced at Reginald to see him stiffen.

"Indeed, Eve. I am sure the lieutenant is brave."

"Enough of me," James insisted. "You must both tell me how you came to know my fair cousin."

Eve nodded. "Up until a year ago we lived quite well in London. Then a reversal of fortune necessitated our relocation to the country. But we are confident that a new venture will soon bring a change of circumstances."

James nodded. "I am happy to hear it."

Eve smiled brightly. "In the meantime, we shall be neighbors. Do you have plans to stay?"

James cast a glance toward Lydia. "I should like to take a country house, somewhere nearby, perhaps."

Eve turned to Lydia. "That would be delightful, would it not? We might all get to know one another so much better."

Lydia wished she could wipe the ingratiating smile from Eve's face. As she watched the girl bob her bright curls, she knew Eve had set her sights upon James. Yet how could she blame her? He was easily the most handsome man Lydia had ever seen. And she had made it clear to Eve, on the evening they discussed him, that she would take no interest in him. Yet now it pained her heart to see the tall, pretty girl using all of her wiles to obtain his heart. But how could she complain? He had made no formal declaration to her. If he favored Eve, how could she dispute his choice?

Her sore heart knew one thing for sure. No matter the outcome between Eve and James, she would never accept Reginald as a suitor, even if her life depended upon it.

Chapter Six

Lydia's dismay deepened when Reginald leaned toward her to say, "Perhaps you and Mr. Summers might like to attend an assembly in the village tonight. It is only a public assembly, but I suppose that cannot be helped."

"Yes. Do come. We could meet you here and ride over together," Eve added.

"I could not possibly," Lydia answered. "You see, Papa is ill, and I dare not leave him, even if he is better tonight."

Reginald raised an eyebrow. "Is he really so ill that you cannot leave?"

"I dare not risk it." Her answer sounded firm, even to her own ears.

Eve turned a pleading face to James. "Then per-

haps Mr. Summers might favor us with his atten-
dance. There shall be other assemblies for Lydia to
attend. And there is always a dreadful shortage of
young men with whom to dance."

James started, looking taken aback. "I could not
go out and leave my uncle. I have promised Miss Lydia that I would be available, should she need me."

Eve quickly masked her disappointment. "You are
most considerate, Mr. Summers. I can only admire
you all the more for keeping to your promise."

Lydia saw through the forced smile, knowing
Eve well enough to believe that she was not at all
happy. And though this plan was thwarted, she would
not easily give up, for Lydia had never met anyone
more determined to get her own way. Once Eve set
her mind on something, she would use all her means
to achieve it as quickly as possible.

Eve turned a sympathetic gaze to Lydia. "If you
should need anything for your poor papa, do not hes-
itate to call upon me. You know how fond I am of the
dear man."

Lydia could not recall Eve's ever professing a particular affection for Papa. In fact, they had rarely
paid the slightest attention to each another. And yet
she could think of no polite way to cast doubt upon
the statement. So she simply said, "I shall remember
your kind offer. I believe, however, that Mr. Summers shall provide all the assistance I could possibly
need."

Eve's piercing blue gaze pinned Lydia like a fly upon paper, issuing a challenge that both women understood. "I am sure you are correct. You may rest easily with Mr. Summers at your service. Still, I hope that, when your papa is well, you will allow Mr. Summers to spread his pleasant company about the village. It would be ungenerous to do otherwise."

Lydia fixed her dark eyes upon Eve's face. "I assure you that Mr. Summers is completely free to do as he chooses."

Reginald spoke in the awkwardness that followed. "I believe it is time for us to depart. We wish your father a speedy return to health, and we shall look forward to our next meeting."

They all stood, and Lydia rang to have the Smyths' wraps brought. When they were bundled into scarves, coats, and capes, Lydia said, "I shall tell Papa that you inquired about his health."

Reginald, hat in hand, gave a bow. "It is kind of you to convey our concern."

Eve added, "Yes, I am sure he suffers greatly. Winter is a terrible time to fall ill."

Lydia shivered at the ominous words.

She was heartened when James said, "Heartiness is a family trait. He will soon be up and well. In the meantime, it was a pleasure to meet both of you."

With nods of farewell, brother and sister swept into the swirling flakes. Eve held herself with the dignity of an ice princess going back to her kingdom.

As the maid closed the door behind them, Lydia was left standing in the portico with James. What must James think of her after meeting Eve? Truly, she was afraid to know. Only an hour ago she had been swept away by their delightful unfolding romance. He had kissed her and held her in his arms. Did he feel the same ardor still for her, or had he been overtaken by Eve's charm?

In spite of her fear, her forthrightness forced her to search his face for an answer. He grinned down. "They seem pleasant enough company, though the brother seems a bit taciturn."

"And the sister?" she asked softly.

He shook his head. "A puzzle. Is she always so gracious and accommodating?"

Lydia wanted to stoutly deny it. Yet she was convinced that denouncing Eve too forcefully would arouse his interest. And that was something she did not want to do.

As mildly as she could mange, she answered, "Eve can be quite charming when she chooses."

James laughed. "I suppose we are all guilty of that trait."

Lydia bit her lip to keep from expressing how especially true it was of Eve. After all, if he truly preferred her, there was little Lydia could do. She had not the disposition to fight Eve at her own game. She refused to simper and flatter, to change who she was in order to win his heart. No, James would choose as he wished. Yet only with Lydia would he know what he was getting.

She pulled herself to her full petite height and said, "Please excuse me. I must be getting up to see Papa. I shall be down for supper at seven o'clock if I can be spared."

With no more said, Lydia clenched her skirt and marched toward the stairs. From the rigid expression on her delicate face, James realized he had said something wrong. He pondered his memory, turning over every word of their conversation, trying to remember if he had said or done anything to regret. Yet, for the life of him, he could not imagine what had caused her distress.

He finally decided that he was must be mistaken. Perhaps she was overcome by a sudden headache, or worry for her papa. Still, she had been very quiet during her neighbors' visit. Perhaps it was Reginald who had upset her. He felt suddenly overcome by a protective instinct. Had Reginald done or said something to discomfit her?

His mind began to entertain a flock of unwelcome thoughts. Had they an understanding before he arrived? If so, perhaps the man's reticence was due to jealousy.

That, he could understand. In the short time he had known the lithe and lovely Lydia, he had fallen for her with all his heart. Was it now to be broken? A wave of jealousy toward Reginald swept over him before his instinct assured him that Lydia would not have allowed him to kiss her if she had no feelings for him. He would not, could not, let himself believe it of her. He made up his mind to obtain a confession from her at the first opportunity. He could not bear not to know her feelings. Even if they lay with Reginald, he was better off knowing before he invested any more of his hopes for their future.

Lydia composed her face into a cheerful mask before knocking on Papa's door. The last thing she wanted to do was to bring her troubles into his sickroom, especially when she had lost her heart to a man he had cautioned her against. She would summon the prudence he always advised and wait for James to reveal his feelings, whether for her or for Eve.

At Papa's murmured invitation, she opened the door and stepped into the room. She could tell at once that he was most unwell. She placed a hand upon his forehead and exclaimed, "You are burning with fever!"

She rang the bell for Sarah, then poured a glass of water from the pitcher beside the bed. Though he tried to wave it away, Lydia helped him hold up his head to take a few sips. When he had drunk the cool liquid, she laid him down gently upon his pillow.

"I am sorry I was not here. I did not know you were so ill again."

Sarah entered, looking surprised as Lydia hissed, "Why did you not come and tell me he was so ill?"

Perplexed, the girl stared at Geoffrey, lying pale upon the pillow.

"He was not so unwell when I brought breakfast this morning. He ate soft eggs and toast and drank all his tea. When I returned for his tray, he was up and about, sitting at his writing desk. I thought it was too soon to be up, but what could I do?"

The girl looked as though she would break into a wail. Not wanting the girl to upset Geoffrey, Lydia softened. "I suppose he has taken a turn for the worse. Bring me rags and a basin of cool water."

"Yes, miss."

Sarah returned, bearing the requested supplies, and Lydia set about sponging her father's hot face and arms. "You will be better soon, Papa."

She spent the afternoon keeping watch on him as he shivered beneath the covers, alternately dozing and waking to complain of the cold. No doubt he had taken a chill from being up and about when he should have been recovering.

"Bring more wood for the fire, Sarah. And tell Mr. Summers that the master has taken a turn for the worse. I shall not be supping with him tonight," she instructed.

Sarah arrived back, bearing an armload of small logs. Geoffrey continued to shiver, though the room was becoming overly warm from the continual blaze. He dozed now and again, awakening occasionally to ramble about the past. He spoke of her mother and times long ago. Lydia treasured his memories, while wishing they could have been imparted under happier circumstances.

She had just dismissed Sarah when he looked straight at Lydia and said, "You have been a good daughter. Your mother would be proud of you. You know, she always loved you as though you were her own."

Lydia frowned. As though she were her own? She tried to make sense of it. Was he delirious? She thought back to the journal. There had been no mention of her birth.

She licked dry lips. "What do you mean, Papa?"

He seemed not to remember the remark. Childhood presents and boyhood games with his brother filled his mind. Lydia bit her lip and tried to think. Her portrait hung in the gallery with the Summer ancestors, all blond and blue eyed. In the back of her mind, the observation had always plagued her. Yet she had succeeded in putting it out of her thoughts. She would no longer be able to do so.

She stood and paced the floor. It was intolerable to sit and worry, with Papa so sick, and now the question of her birth lying before her. She wrung her hands and redoubled her prayers for Papa's recovery.

If he worsened and died, the answer would die with him.

She stayed to watch over him all through the long evening hours. Sarah brought her a tray of lamb and potatoes and conveyed Mr. Summers' concern for her father. Her thoughts were in too much confusion to give much thought to James.

"Tell him I am grateful. And, Sarah, bring some broth for my father. I shall try to see if he will take a little."

"Yes, miss." Sarah glanced at Geoffrey with concern before departing.

Lydia found that she could eat only a few bites. What little she ate stuck in her throat and churned in her stomach. Instead, she bathed her father's head, then sat back while he slept. She studied the heavy brocade curtains patterned with leaves of ivy. They shut out the dark and cold of night as surely as she had been shut away from her past. She shivered, wondering if she would ever know the truth.

Only once did Geoffrey rouse long enough for her to coax a spoonful of broth into his mouth. She was on the verge of sending James for the doctor, when he settled into a deep sleep. She felt his forehead to find that he was cooler. She settled back in the plush, mint-colored bedside chair and allowed herself to doze.

She awoke in the very early morning to find that Sarah had kept the fire ablaze all night. Geoffrey had tossed back his covers, and Lydia found him cool to her touch. He awoke and stared at her with a lucid gaze, despite the dark circles under his eyes.

"It is very warm in here, is it not?"

Lydia smiled at him. "Your fever has broken. You were chilled last night, so Sarah kept up the fire."

"I feel much better—hungry, in fact."

"That is good news. I shall ring for your breakfast."

"And yours too. You look weary. Have you been here all night with me?"

She nodded. "I could not have stayed away. You were so very ill."

He patted her hand. "You are a good daughter. Better than I have deserved."

She licked her lips and forced herself to ask the question that she both dreaded and longed to have answered. "When you were ill last night, you told me that Mama had loved me as her own. Please, I must know. If I am not truly her child, whose am I?"

Geoffrey looked away. "She never wanted you to know. But when it seemed I might die, it seemed only right that you should know the truth."

Lydia clenched her hands in her lap and waited for him to continue.

"We could not have children. After eight years of marriage, we still had not had a child. Mariah was very fond of her young maid. When the girl became with child, the father abandoned her, and Mariah refused to turn her from the house. The girl had the babe right here in this room. It was a beautiful, raven-haired girl, part Gypsy, like her mother. Olive skin and black almond eyes."

Lydia felt tears welling in her eyes. She stared at the man she had always called Papa and knew now why he had paid little attention to her as a child. He had allowed her to stay on, believing herself to be his daughter for the sake of Mariah.

He shook his head. "The mother died in childbirth, and Mariah vowed to keep you and rear you as her own. She doted on you, even naming you after her mother. You filled her need for a child. For that I am grateful."

"You kept me on all these years for the sake of Mama. But what of your own feelings? How you must have despised me."

He drew back with surprise. "I am not a demonstrative man, Lydia, and I was often busy, but I never despised you."

Lydia's mind refused to accept the assurance. She had learned from reading stories that some children's fathers brought presents when returning from a trip. In spite of her excitement when Geoffrey returned home, she often went two or three days without seeing him. And now she knew. She was not his child at all. She was a charity, a burden, born on the wrong side of the blanket.

The truth stabbed like an unbearable wound. She

wished she had never been told. But there could be no going back now, no fooling herself into believing that she belonged. She was an imposter, with no right to ask anything of any servant in the house. No doubt any one of them had a better birthright than her own.

She rose, stifling a flood of tears. "I must go now. I am glad you are better."

He called to her. "I hope I have done the right thing."

She could not answer. Overwhelmed by a flood of tears, Lydia dashed down the hall to her chambers and locked her door. She threw herself upon the pale chenille spread and wept, not only for the past, but for what it would mean to her future.

When her tears were spent at last, she lay upon the bed and wondered how she would ever face James again. The memory of his kiss, so precious before, now seared her like a burn. What would he think of her if he knew the truth? Well, that was one thing she would never reveal. She could not bear the pain of seeing disdain replace the affection in his eyes.

Some hours later Sarah rapped upon her door. "Shall I help you dress for supper, miss?"

"No, thank you, Sarah. I shall not be coming down."

"Yes, miss. I shall bring up a tray."

"I do not need a tray, Sarah. I am not hungry."

"Yes, miss."

She heard Sarah's concern yet was beyond caring.

Even if she had been hungry, she would be uncomfortable ever being served again in this house. As soon as possible, she would earn her own keep, and Geoffrey would be free of any responsibility for her. No doubt it was what he had wanted for years, she thought miserably.

The fire burned low in the grate, and she began to shiver. She crawled under the covers and sunk, at last, into the oblivion of sleep. Each time she roused, she squeezed her eyes closed to shut out her thoughts until the anemic sun fought its way into the sky.

She opened her eyes, knowing it was useless to try to sleep. In the inky cover of night she could almost pretend that it was all a dream, that morning would set everything to rights. Now daylight had come and harshly stripped away any foggy-brained hope of rescue. No knight in armor could take away her curse, and she dared not hope that any would care to try. She was tainted and stained by a choice not her own, and no motherly love could reach beyond the grave to remove it.

If she could convince Geoffrey to go along with the story of her being his daughter just a little longer, she felt sure she could obtain a position as a governess, as far away from Holly Green Manor as she could manage. She was well educated and fond of children. Surely that would be enough to recommend her.

She lay staring at the ceiling, as weak fingers

of sunlight attempted to reach into the room. The comforts around her that she had always taken for granted now made her feel *un*comfortable. Her soft bed made up with immaculate white linen, her tall wardrobe filled with stylish clothing, plentiful food, and servants to tend to the housework. By all rights she belonged in the poorhouse. But how bitter to have grown up with the privileges of the gentry, only to discover it was all a charade.

She swung her feet to the floor and consoled herself with the thought that, of all women to meet such misfortune, she was a better choice than most. She did not live for the comforts of life, nor did she care overly much about the benefits of society. If she could conceal the unhappy truth from James and the Smyths, she could leave with her pride intact. She prayed to be spared the torture of seeing Eve's gloating or Reginald's loathing should they discover the truth. Position was everything to them. The fact that Eve felt that her own current circumstances were far below what she deserved would make her all the haughtier.

She dressed and rang for breakfast, though the action gave her pause. Nonetheless, she could hardly join the kitchen staff while in this house, for to do so would cause an endless stream of gossip, gossip that she did not want to deflect.

When she heard a knock at her door, she assumed it was Sarah with her tray. She bid her enter, only to discover that Papa stood in the doorway, a blanket pulled tightly about his gaunt body. Fear for his health brought her to her feet.

"You should not be out of bed. The last time you did this, you caught a terrible chill."

"I am all better now, and this is a very warm blanket. I had to see you, Lydia. I am sorry for the way I told you about your parentage last night. I did not mean to cause you grief."

Lydia lowered her eyes. "It is better that I know."

Geoffrey stepped into the room and shut the door before settling into the armchair beside the large oval mirror. He sighed wearily and said, "I was never good with words like Mariah. She would have known not to blurt out the truth. I know that I shocked you. And for that, I am heartily sorry."

"You need not apologize. It seems I owe you more than I ever imagined. However, that does not change the truth. I have given it a great deal of thought. If you will only refrain from telling anyone for a while, perhaps I may obtain a position as governess. Once I am employed, you will be free of the obligation imposed upon you by your wife."

Hot tears welled in her eyes, infuriating and embarrassing her. She had been determined to maintain her composure when facing Geoffrey, not offering him the satisfaction of knowing how deeply it hurt to know that he must be relieved to be rid of her at last. Even being cast adrift without a family caused her less pain than the knowledge that she had strived to love a father who had loathed her in return.

It surprised her when Geoffrey brushed away his own tears and said, "Oh, Lydia. What have I done?" He sniffed and said, "I never meant for you to leave. You are all I have in the world. You kept me alive all these years when I would have let go. And I knew Mariah would not have wanted you to grow up without me. So you see, you gave me a reason to live."

He paused for a breath. "At first, when Mariah was gone, I was resentful of you. It was unfair that she had died, leaving me with a child that was not our own. For years I stayed so busy that I fear I neglected you most terribly. But in these last few months since you have been home, I have realized what a kind and intelligent young woman you have become. No daughter could have taken better care of me when I was ill. In every way that counts, you are my daughter. I love having you in my life."

Could it be that he actually had fatherly feelings for her? She would never have thought it possible. Yet the tears that shone in his pale blue eyes convinced her otherwise. How ironic that after all these years of trying to win his affection, he gave it now when it would not be fair to him to accept it.

"I will be a burden to you if I stay. I cannot marry a gentleman. I should be lucky to marry a tenant. And such a match could only be an embarrassment to you."

Geoffrey frowned. "And why should you not marry a gentleman? I would die before I would tell anyone about your circumstances. Your pretty face will win you a suitable match. That is all that I ask from life now. To see you safely settled, well, and happy. Then I may die a contented man."

"Do you believe I could stand to wed in deception? Even if my husband never found out, I would feel such a shame that I would tell him myself."

Geoffrey shook his head. "There is no need. You are no less the person, the lady, than you were last week, or yesterday evening, before my ill-planned revelation."

Lydia caught a glimpse of herself in the mirror, her dark eyes full of grief. She swallowed hard and said, "And yet, I do not feel like the same person."

"Give it time. Please, for my sake, if you can forgive my past neglect, do not go away. You are my daughter in every way that counts. I shall die of grief if you leave me like this."

Lydia felt a cleansing wave of pity well in her chest. He longed for company now that he was alone and in ill health. It would be ungrateful and heartless to leave him now after he had provided for her all these years. She would stay and do her best to play the part that now seemed a burden.

She looked into his desperate face and replied, "I will stay if you wish. I am not ungrateful for all you have done for me."

Geoffrey harrumphed. "You owe me nothing. It is I who have benefited."

She smiled at him, her heart warmed by words of affection she had waited all her life to hear.

Geoffrey pushed to his feet. "Let us say no more about this. You be about your breakfast, and then join me in the drawing room. I cannot bear another day spent in bed."

He leaned over the bed, and she kissed his thin cheek. "I shall be right along."

She joined him after dressing and pulling her hair into a sleek chignon. She ate breakfast with him without tasting a bite of her food. Her lot in life was now laid fully before her. She would stay on here until Geoffrey died and hope that the pension he left her would allow her to survive until she might find employment.

James was out of her reach now. She could only pray that God would give her the strength to endure James' marriage to another woman. Eve, perhaps. For surely he would marry and, one day, bring his wife to this house.

The revelation of her heredity had brought so much pain that she wished she had never been born. And yet, knowing in her sturdy heart that this was something she could not undo, she determined to endure it.

Her resolve wavered slightly upon arriving in the drawing room to see James sitting on the settee, enjoying the warmth of the fire. He turned an admiring glance upon her, giving her the half smile she had come to love.

She turned her gaze away, trying to ignore the painful ache in her chest. She had survived before she knew him, and she would continue to draw breath without him. She only hoped that time would erase the memories etched so firmly in her mind.

Chapter Seven

She felt Geoffrey scrutinizing her face as he said, "I was just telling James how important it is to have someone who is devoted to you in your old age. Any of the servants could have nursed me, but it is not the same as someone who truly cares for you."

Lydia forced a smile, hoping he had not broken his promise and told James about her birth. The very thought made her feel ill. She paused, resting her hand upon the door frame, unsure whether to continue into the room. If James were to discover the truth, she would go far away where she need never face him again.

She inclined her head, and Geoffrey read the question in her eyes. He shook his head, and she let out a breath of relief. On weak legs she crossed the plush

Asian rug to one of the chairs beside the settee. The newly acquired burden that had buried itself deep in her heart made her feel ill at ease as she groped for a topic of conversation.

She turned her attention to Geoffrey. "Are you sure you are warm enough?"

Geoffrey turned to James. "See? Is it not as I said, this concern she has for me?"

To Lydia, he said, "My dear, I am quite comfortable."

She settled back into her chair and tried to relax.

James smiled at her. "I spent yesterday afternoon taking a brisk ride. I met one of your tenants—a Mr. Barker, I believe. He told me how kind you were last summer when his wife was ill. You came every day to bring food and to care for the children. He said he could not have tended to his crops if not for you."

Lydia felt the warmth rise in her cheeks. "Mr. Barker is exaggerating. I did no more than anyone else would have done had they known about his troubles."

James raised an eyebrow. "You would be surprised how blind most of us can be when it comes to those in need. We often see only what we want and ignore what might disturb our comfortable world."

Lydia shivered. "Up until recently my world was my school in London. I never saw the needs that surely existed in the poorer parts of the city."

She wondered how many babies, orphaned like

herself, had not the benefit of someone such as Mariah Summers. Those children suffered in want and cold on the harsh streets of the city, far away from the fine school she had attended. She had never thought about it back then, never wondered how those in the orphanages or the poorhouses were faring.

She determined that if she had the means to do so, she would like to assist those in need someday. With a leap of her heart, she realized that she would like to repay Mama by taking a child from an orphanage and giving that small boy or girl a chance for a better life.

She sighed. The pension Papa would leave would be adequate for her to live a frugal life. However, it would leave little left for the rearing of a child.

She started when James asked, "Why so pensive? With your Papa feeling better and hardly a cloud in our bright blue sky, I would think to see a smile gracing your lips."

Lydia shook her head. "It is nothing. Would you like tea? I could ring for some."

"Not for me, thank you," James replied.

Lydia licked her lips and asked, "For you, Papa?"

"No, thank you. I had a cup at breakfast."

James flipped through the pages of a book that was lying in his lap. "I wonder if it would be presumptuous to impose a bit of reading upon you both. I would like to improve my skill and would welcome criticism toward that end."

Lydia's heart skipped a beat. He had remembered his promise to read aloud. It had sounded romantic when they had spoken that day in the library. Now a lump formed in her throat as she imagined what might have been. Were it not for her low birth, James might have extended a proposal, which she could accept, and, when wed, she would have been privileged to have this fine man read to her on many a winter day. Now there could be no such hope. Her dreams were as cold as the ashes on a midnight grate.

Nonetheless, she could hardly explain her lessened enthusiasm. There was nothing to be done save nod and say, "That would be lovely, would it not, Papa?"

"Indeed, I should like nothing better."

Geoffrey settled contentedly beneath his blanket as though all that had been wrong had been set right. He closed his eyes and nodded as James began to read the words of a poet describing his feelings upon lingering in a churchyard.

Lydia stared into the fire and tried to conceal the anguish that swept through her. Never had she heard a man read with such fine passion, as though he were the poet himself, experiencing firsthand all that the scene evoked.

In torture, she endured the resonance of his voice, biting her lip when her throat choked and tears welled in her eyes. She would not cry. She would learn to control the feelings that James evoked.

He finished the poem and looked over at her as he held his place in the book. She met his intense gaze and forced a bright smile. "That was lovely. I cannot think of a single comment to improve your reading."

He grinned, stabbing her heart with the warmth in his eyes. "That *is* kind. I have spent too little effort in practicing aloud to deserve such acclaim."

Geoffrey opened one eye. "Pray, continue. I have not heard good poetry in a very long time."

James opened the book and obliged with a second poem. Again Lydia felt her heart react to the timbre of his voice, luring and enticing, bathing her with a passion that she could never accept.

When James finished the poem, Geoffrey stirred and opened his eyes. He nodded his approval. "You have given us a fine performance, has he not, Lydia?"

"Yes, very fine," she agreed.

Geoffrey rose slowly, grasping the armrests with the weakness of an invalid. "I would stay and hear more, but I must admit to the need for a nap. So I shall leave you to enjoy the fire and more reading if you wish."

Lydia stirred. "I shall help you to your chambers."

He held up a hand to stop her. "No. You have done enough for me when I needed your ministrations. Now I am perfectly able to make my way back to my bed."

She watched his slow progress until he disappeared into the hallway. With his withdrawal, her discomfort was complete. The last thing she wanted was to be alone with James.

In desperation she rose and said, "I must be seeing to the day's menu. Papa will need something nourishing for dinner."

He caught her arm as she attempted to escape. "By all means, see to the menu. But when you finish, will you not return? It is a perfect day for a ride through the woods to a lovely little park at the edge of your fields. I discovered it yesterday."

She avoided his eyes. "I cannot. I have a headache. Perhaps another time."

He released her arm. "Have I said or done something to upset you?"

The sincerity of his question forced her to meet his gaze, an effort that cost her dearly. "No. Please forgive me. It is nothing you have done. It is entirely me."

She turned away and fled.

James had seen the tears welling in Lydia's eyes. He watched in helpless misery as all his hopes for the day sank like a ship crippled in battle. He longed to follow her, yet he dared not do so. Had she not made it clear that it was his company she wished to avoid?

What had he done? He thought back to their last encounter. Only yesterday they had walked together. He had kissed her, and she had responded with a warmth that encouraged his dreams. He had been sure things between them were going quite well. And then Eve and Reginald had come to visit, and Lydia had gone quiet.

Suddenly it struck him. That had to be it. Something about the visit had caused her grief. Could Reginald have upset her? Or perhaps . . . had he paid too much attention to Eve? He had not meant to do so. Perhaps Lydia feared that his attachment was threatened by her comely acquaintance. The thought made him uneasy. Eve had seemed taken with him; he had thought so at the time. But he had dismissed the notion. She was not at all the sort of girl to tempt his affections. Nothing about her compared to the fresh charm of Lydia. Why, it was like comparing a hothouse flower to a fresh garden rose.

Yet Lydia knew none of this. He would have to convince her. He could not bear the thought of having her worry even for a moment over the steadiness of his affection. Now that he knew the reason for her behavior, he longed to put things right. He set off to find her, sure that a few moments alone would restore their former closeness.

He inquired of the butler and was told that Miss Summers had just set off for the stables. It was as he had suspected. Her headache was merely an excuse. He grabbed his riding coat and hat and hurried off to find her.

He rounded the corner of the path and saw her disappear into the stables. He hurried his steps and called to her. By the time he entered and the young groom bid him good day, Lydia was nowhere in sight.

James frowned. "Miss Summers—where has she gone?"

The boy fiddled with the harness he had in his hands. Avoiding James' eyes, he said, "I do'n know, sir. 'Aven't seen her."

Exasperated, James took a step toward the boy. "She just walked into the stables."

The boy stared at the ground. "Sorry, sir."

He gave up on getting information from the groom and decided to perform his own search. He walked the length of the stalls, glancing into each one. He reached an empty stall and peered down. She was so petite that he never would have seen her crouching against the door, if not for the telltale hem of her riding skirt.

"Lydia?"

James pushed up the latch of the half door. "Are you hiding from me?"

She popped up, cheeks red and almond eyes full of guilt. "Hiding from you? Of course not. Why should I be hiding from you?"

"That is what I should like to know, though I believe I have guessed the reason."

Lydia turned pale. "I hope not, for if you have, I shall not be able to face you."

He clasped her cold hands. "My darling, it is Eve, is it not? You believe that I fancy her. But I have come to assure you of my unaltered affection toward you. Please do not believe that I could be tempted by anyone else now that I have met you, for you are all that I could ever want."

Lydia choked on a sob as she laughed. "I did worry that you might be persuaded toward Eve. Now I wish that it were only that simple, for that is something I might have altered."

James rested his back against the stable wall as he pulled her to his chest. He longed to give her comfort. The fragrance of lilac perfumed her hair, drifting up to him to compete with the smells of tack and hay, horses and saddle soap. He wished he could hold her always and protect her from whatever was causing her pain.

Baffled, he said, "I must admit my confusion. If it is not Eve, then what has come between us? Reginald, perhaps?"

She dug for her lace kerchief in the pocket of her riding coat. Dabbing at her nose, she said, "Reginald is no more than a pompous bother."

James frowned. "Then what?"

She shook her head. "I cannot tell you. I will not tell you."

He kissed the top of her head. "It cannot be so terrible."

Lydia pulled away. Eyes bright with tears, she cried, "It is more horrible than you can imagine. If you knew the truth, you would not be standing with me now. So, please, be kind to us both and take no more notice of me."

With those ominous words, she turned and ran from the stables. James watched her in stunned disbelief. What had come over her? He could not imagine anything so disastrous as to deserve this strong reaction. Whatever was wrong could surely be resolved. He followed her from the stables, determined to find an answer. If not from Lydia, then from the old master of the manor.

He did not have a chance to speak to Geoffrey until after supper. Lydia made a hasty retreat after the meal, claiming yet another headache. Since she did look a bit pale, James made no objection but seized the opportunity of her absence to ask Geoffrey, "Please, sir. Lydia has not been herself of late. I thought I knew the reason, but I was wrong. I must admit to a particular fondness for her, and I will go crazy if I do not know what is the matter."

Geoffrey toyed with his glass of wine, watching as he swirled the amber liquid. After a moment of deliberation, he asked. "Do you believe that Lydia shares an affection for you?"

"I do. Or at least I did believe it. To be honest, sir, I had hoped, in time, to win her hand in marriage."

Geoffrey sighed. "It would be with misgivings that I would give my consent. Do you not realize the danger you could put her in if you persist in courting her? There is a curse on this family, a curse on the heir. If he does not die, then it is someone he loves. I do not wish for it to be Lydia."

"Neither do I. But I do not believe there is a curse. If there was foul play in the past, it is done with now. I care for Lydia, and I believe she cares for me, and I do not want to sacrifice our chance for happiness."

Geoffrey plunked down his glass. "Are you not listening, man? Murder has plagued every generation since my uncle died. Are you not at all worried that it may claim you too?"

James shook his head. "Even if I were, I would not let those circumstances rule my life."

Geoffrey's frail shoulders slumped as he said, "Then I see that I have no choice other than to break my promise, for it may be the only way to keep you and Lydia apart."

James felt his palms grow damp as he waited for Geoffrey to reveal the terrible secret. He could not imagine anything that would make him part from Lydia. And yet the anguish on the older man's face revealed a deeply concealed and closely guarded burden upon his heart.

He listened in silence as Geoffrey described his marriage to Mariah and her pain in not bearing a child. By the time he told of how the young maid delivered the babe, he knew that it was Lydia. A momentary shock washed over him before he realized that he did not care. Whatever the circumstances of her birth, she had been raised a lady, and a lady she would always be. If she thought him capable of withdrawing his affection because she had not the pure blood and deep blue eyes of his forebearers, she would find herself mistaken. And though he cared little for the approval of society, did not care if Prince Prinny himself knew, for her benefit he would keep her secret.

And as no inheritance stipulations rested upon his marriage, he had no one to please except himself. If he wished to marry a peasant or a match girl or a girl born to an unmarried lass, it was his own business. Surely Geoffrey could not mean for her to shut herself away, forever denied a husband because of a past she had no choice in creating.

When he stated those sentiments, Geoffrey shook his head and said, "Of course I want her to wed. And I have no personal objections to you, as you seem a decent chap. I hoped her background would dissuade you only because of the danger you may bring to her."

Geoffrey scowled, bringing his gray eyebrows together. "I hope you will have the gentlemanly manners to keep her past in confidence when she does settle on a suitable match. You see, she is fearful to marry, believing that it would be a disaster should her husband somehow discover her circumstances of birth."

"Then she should be relieved that she will not have that worry with me, as I would go into the match already knowing her past and accepting her in spite of it. As to the danger we may face, I believe it is something that Lydia should decide for herself. If she does not want to take the risk with me, then I shall not pursue this match. However, if she chooses of her own free will, will you not respect her choice?"

Geoffrey sat up straight in alarm. "You do not mean to tell her that I have broken her confidence? I forbid it, for she will turn you away and never forgive me. And then she will go away. If you would have such poor judgment as to pursue her now, then I forbid you to speak to her. If you will not promise to remain silent, you must leave immediately."

James felt as though his heart were on fire. How could he be expected to sit here and make a promise that would deny both himself and Lydia their futures? How could her father not feel that her happiness was worth taking this chance?

Shaking his head, James said, "I cannot promise not to speak to her. In fact, even if you send me away, I shall find a way, sooner or later, to assure her of my unchanged affection."

"Then you are stubborn and selfish. You refuse to take Lydia's best interest to heart. Therefore I can no longer welcome you as a guest in my home. For you see, this is still my house."

"I am aware of that, sir, and I will not presume upon your hospitality if you wish me to leave. Just remember that I shall not abandon Lydia."

With that, James stood and, with a bow, removed himself from the room. He made his way up the stairs and paused at Lydia's door. Dare he intrude upon her solitude to express his devotion? Seized by desperation, he knocked upon her door.

He was bid to enter, only to find her sitting at her dressing table with her head resting upon the hard wood. He strode into the room and paused beside her. Kneeling beside her slumped shoulders, he said, "Lydia, I have come to speak to you."

When she made no reply, he touched her gently upon the shoulder.

"Are you all right?"

When she still did not reply, he touched her cheek and found that she was burning with fever. His heart lurched with fear as he swept her into his arms and laid her upon her bed. Her eyes flicked open and rested upon his face.

She whispered hoarsely, "I wish I could tell you why I can no longer see you, but you would despise me if I did."

He kissed her forehead and said, "I already know, my love. Your father has told me everything, and I do not care. I love you, and I always will."

He straightened and said, "I must ring for Sarah, for you need to be properly put to bed. Promise me you will get well soon."

Lydia smiled drowsily and said, "I promise."

She had drifted to sleep by the time he rang for the

maid. He remained by Lydia's side until she arrived to undress her mistress.

"Stay with her and care for her. I shall check in later to see how she is doing."

"I will, sir. She must've caught whatever the master had."

James sighed. "You are probably right."

As he went back down to tell Geoffrey of her illness, he assured himself that Lydia was young and strong. She would quickly recover. And yet the fear that plucked at the back of his mind made him determined that, in order to be close to her, he would sleep in the lane if Geoffrey threw him from the house.

Geoffrey had retired to the drawing room, ensconced by the cozy fire, eyes closed as he sipped his brandy. James trod into the room, prepared to beg if necessary in order to stay.

Geoffrey heard his steps and opened his eyes. His pale brow pulled into a frown as he said, "I have not changed my mind. We have nothing more to discuss."

"I have not come on that matter. I have discovered that Lydia is burning with fever. Perhaps she caught whatever ailed you. I summoned Sarah to care for her."

Geoffrey pushed himself from his chair. "I shall go at once to check on her. If she becomes too ill, we shall need the doctor."

"Then you do not mind if I stay until her recovery is certain?"

"Not if you can be of use."

With no more ado, James followed Geoffrey up the stairs. Sarah admitted them into Lydia's chamber. Any concern Geoffrey felt about James' presence in his daughter's room was overshadowed by his concern for her health. He sat on the edge of the bed and took her hand.

"Lydia, can you hear me?"

Her eyelids flickered. Dark lashes brushed her fever-flushed cheeks. She was too drowsy to reply.

Geoffrey patted her hand.

"Watch over her tonight, Sarah. Wake me immediately if she takes a turn for the worse."

"Yes, sir."

"Keep sponging her with cool water. Perhaps it will help with the fever," James said.

Sarah nodded.

Geoffrey rose with a tired sigh. "I shall sleep for a while so that I can sit with her in the morning."

James lingered until Geoffrey said, "Come then. I shall summon you if we have need of the doctor."

He followed Geoffrey into the hall and waited until he shut the door to his chambers. Then he slipped back to be with Lydia. He sat in the chair beside the bed and took her hand, rubbing her fingers softly with his thumb. Alternately he dozed and awoke, touching her hot cheek in the hope that the fever would break.

Just before dawn she stirred restlessly. James opened his eyes to see that Sarah had fallen asleep on the end of the bed. He leaned forward and touched Lydia's cheek. She felt noticeably cooler. He let out the breath he was holding.

She opened her eyes, focused on his face, and smiled. Whispering through parched lips, she asked, "Have you been here all night?"

"I have. I was worried about you."

She smiled. "You must not worry. I shall be well soon. How is Papa?"

"Improving still. He was worried about you last night. He plans to sit with you today."

She protested with a weak shake of her head. "He must not overtax his strength."

"And neither shall you. I intend to stay close by and make sure you rest for the next few days."

"I do not deserve your kindness."

"Did you not hear what I told you last night? I know, and I do not care."

Lydia blinked back tears. "I thought it was a dream."

He squeezed her hand gently. "It was no dream. I do not care anything about your heredity. In India I knew women of the best breeding who would not tempt me in the slightest. You, my sweet and spirited

Lydia, are the woman I love. And if you turn me down, I shall sit under your window and pine away until you change your mind."

She smiled through her tears. "You really do not care?"

He raised her hand to impart a kiss. "Not in the slightest. It is nothing to me."

"If anyone were to find out, it would ruin your place in society."

"They will not. And if they did, I assure you that I care more for you than any place in society."

"You are too good. But what of children? I would never condemn them to a life of being ostracized."

"If the worst happens, we shall all move to India. Nothing would be known about us there."

Lydia attempted to lick her lips. "I shall think about it."

Sarah roused, and James said, "Your mistress is awake. Go and fetch her a cool drink of water."

The girl shook off her sleepiness and hurried to comply. She returned with a glass of water, and together she and James raised Lydia to help her drink. When her thirst had been slacked, she fell again into an exhausted sleep.

James watched her, thinking that her finely chiseled face looked like a porcelain doll's, delicately and painstakingly made to be breathtakingly beautiful. At last he stirred himself to tell Sarah, "I am going down for some breakfast. When she awakens, make sure she has some porridge to eat."

He was eager to tell Geoffrey of Lydia's improvement and ease the man's mind. And yet he knew it would mean his withdrawal forthwith from the house. Nonetheless, he would find nearby residence while he awaited Lydia's contemplation of his informal proposal. And with all of his heart, he prayed her answer would be yes.

Chapter Eight

Now that he felt assured of Lydia's improvement, James found that he could eat a hearty breakfast. He welcomed the eggs and sausage and strong black tea that the butler set before him. He sated his appetite on all of these, along with flaky hot rolls streaming with creamy butter.

With his appetite appeased, he felt prepared to face Geoffrey, to tell him that he would never be persuaded that he and Lydia were not meant for each other. He would wait for her, if need be, but he would not give her up.

"Has the master rung for breakfast?" he asked the butler.

"No, sir. He has neither come down nor requested his breakfast."

James nodded. He wiped his mouth with his napkin and arose. He wanted to speak to Geoffrey yet would not dream of disturbing his privacy, of waking him without there being a true crisis at hand.

He trod up the stairs, hoping to discover the gentleman on his way down for breakfast. Instead, he found Sarah heading for Geoffrey's open door.

"Is he up?" James asked.

"Yes, sir. He is in with the mistress. I thought I should slip in and straighten his room."

James shook his head. "You go and get yourself some breakfast straightaway. I know you have been with Miss Lydia all night and have not had a chance to eat. You can straighten the room later."

Sarah curtseyed. "Thank you, sir. That is kind."

He sighed, imagining what Geoffrey would think of him if he heard him ordering the servants as though it were already his house. Someday it would be, and when it was, he looked forward to rearing a whole new generation of Summers children. And he intended to do it with Lydia as his wife.

He lingered in the hall until Geoffrey left Lydia's room. The older man scowled when he saw him and said, "It was wrong of you to run straightaway and tell her. It could have brought disaster. Now she is saying, 'I love him, Papa, and he loves me.' She is too young to understand the risks of this love."

"Perhaps my declaration took a great weight off

her shoulders. Did you not find her in improved health and spirits?"

"I did. I suppose now that she has met you, she will not be happy without you." Face drawn, he added, "The matter is out of my hands. God be with you both."

It was clear that illness and worry had taken a toll on Geoffrey's ill-maintained health. James hoped that he might be a part of restoring a little of the gentleman's faith in life. A home full of laughter and the prattle of children would surely stir him out of himself. He looked into blue eyes that were so like his own and asked, "Mariah chose to marry you. Surely she knew the story of the family past."

Geoffrey shuddered. "She did. We were so in love, we could not believe that the past could hurt us. And now I see it happening all over again."

James clasped his uncle's shoulder. "The past is buried, Uncle. You will see."

"It matters not what I think. Lydia is too headstrong for me to forbid. Stay as long as you like and court her."

His shoulders slumped in resignation as he plodded down the stairs. James imagined he would hole up in the drawing room to think up all the dire consequences to come. And though he was heartily sorry for Geoffrey, he could not help being elated by Lydia's declaration of love.

He rapped on her door. Now that there were no

more secrets, there was nothing to stop their wedding.

At her invitation, he stepped inside. She sat propped upon her pillows, wearing a soft pink bed jacket that complimented the pale pink in her cheeks. He longed to take her into his arms and smother her with kisses. Yet he had been careful to leave the door open to preserve her reputation, which meant that a servant might walk in upon them at any time.

"How are you feeling, my love?"

Lydia smiled, loving the endearment. "A little tired but much improved."

"You are to spend the whole day in bed, resting and drinking tea. And you shall not get up until you are completely recovered."

"And who will determine when I am recovered?"

James was pleased to see a little of the old fire in her eyes.

"I believe you are sufficiently capable of making that decision."

She smiled, chagrined to know she had risen to his bait. "I believe I am, at that." She stifled a yawn and asked. "And will you spend the day with me?"

James shook his head. "I must find a house to let. It is not right for me to think up upon your father any longer. Yet you may be assured that I shall come to see you every single day."

"He does not approve of this match. Still, I wish you would not go."

He took her hand and turned it over to gently kiss her palm. "I fear I must. I will come back later in the afternoon, after you have had a good rest, and I will tell you what I have found."

"I would like that," she said. She longed to keep him with her. Yet fatigue from her illness claimed her too quickly. Her eyelids flickered as she nodded off to sleep. James laid her hand gently upon the bed before departing soundlessly from the room.

Lydia awoke at midday. The headache that had plagued her was gone, and she was hungry. As she ate her light dinner of creamed potatoes and tea, she wondered whether James had been able to locate a suitable residence. It seemed silly to her that he was moving out. He loved her and she him. They would be married soon, perhaps in the middle of spring. And then he would live in this house again with her and Papa, for she felt sure that Papa would want them here.

Her pleasant thoughts were interrupted as Sarah announced a visitor. "Miss Smyth to see you, miss."

Since Eve slipped into the room before Lydia had a chance to reply, there would be no getting around the visit. Perhaps it was for the best, she decided. A visit from Eve might be just what she needed to stir her blood.

Eve clucked her tongue. "Sarah tells me you have been ill. Indeed, you do look rather wan. It is most inconsiderate of you to get sick on a dreary day when I long to take a walk. I am so tired of being cooped up in the house."

Though her tone was teasing, Lydia did not doubt that Eve was displeased to have her plans disrupted. She had obviously dressed to be seen, in a pale blue organdy that complemented her eyes. Her hair was braided into a shining coil atop her head, while pale ringlets framed her face.

She perched in the chair beside Lydia's bed. The pink of the upholstery brought out the color in her cheeks, leaving Lydia to admit that Eve was everything she was not. Tall, blond, and fair, she looked as though she belonged in this family. It gave Lydia another pang in her heart to remember that she did not.

"Where is Mr. James Summers? Perhaps he would not be averse to taking a turn with me if you cannot."

So that was it, Lydia realized. This visit was for the purpose of winning the heart of her very own James. Eve had come dressed and coiffed to win his admiration and lure him into her grasp. Lydia smiled sweetly at her friend, well-pleased to be able to tell her that she was too late to achieve her goal.

"I have a secret that I know I may trust with you."

Eve leaned toward Lydia, her eyes wide with interest. "Of course. I am the soul of discretion."

"Mr. Summers and I have come to an arrangement. You see, we have fallen in love, and we plan to marry."

It took a moment for Eve to erase the shock and dismay that showed upon her handsome features. "But, Lydia, you do not want to marry him. He is not at all right for you."

"Why is that?"

It was obvious that Eve was trying to think of a good answer. She patted Lydia's hand. "Think, dear. You are much too impetuous. You have been swept away by his charm. You do not want a man who is as impulsive as Mr. Summers. When he becomes bored, he will leave you for his next adventure. And I do not want to see you left brokenhearted and alone. Mr. Summers requires a woman who knows how to handle him, someone sophisticated and clever with men."

"Someone like you?"

Eve cocked an eyebrow. "Perhaps. The truth is, you would never be able to hold him. I know how to handle a man such as James Summers. So why should I not have him?"

Lydia was incensed. "Because he is pledged to me."

Eve sat back and fixed Lydia with a cool stare. "I tell you these things because of our friendship. Your best decision would be to marry Reginald. He seems taken with you. If you refuse my advice and stay bent on your course, you will be sorry. Yet I know how dreadfully stubborn you can be."

Lydia sat up straight against her pillows. "The

truth is that you do not want to lose a chance to better yourself. You see Mr. Summers as a way to become mistress of an estate. That is all that he is to you, and you are angry because he prefers me."

Eve's blue eyes darkened with anger. "How dare you insult me, you little twit? You have no idea what you are up against."

"Apparently you have no faith in the power of love."

"Love does not give one a proper home or a place in society. You do not understand such things because you have never been in want. I tell you out of friendship that you should take Reginald while he will have you."

"Never. I do not love Reginald, and I do not believe that he loves me. We would make each other miserable for the rest of our lives."

"That is unfortunate indeed. My advice has been for your benefit. But it seems you will have none of it. So I shall take my leave with a clear conscience and console myself with the knowledge that I did my best for the sake of our friendship."

Eve pulled herself from the chair with regal grace. Her features were etched with disdain as she stared down upon Lydia. With a shake of her head, she turned and stalked out the door.

Lydia felt as though she had been in a battle. She sank upon her pillows, feeling weak and exhausted All the energy she had gained had been lost in the skirmish. How could Eve not realize that Lydia could see through her self-serving interest?

Posh, she thought. Eve must think she was a simpleton indeed if she accepted the lie that Eve was putting Lydia's interest first. No, indeed. She wanted the position that being mistress of the estate would bring. Trips to London, finer clothes. She would bleed the estate dry and never care.

It would not happen. It must not happen. James loved her, and she loved him. That was the way it would stay. She would put all of Eve's silly words from her head and not give them another thought.

Yet when she drifted back to sleep, her dreams were troubled by visions of Eve and James laughing together, walking together. She tried to join them, and neither of them paid her any mind. She sobbed so long and hard that she awoke feeling more drained than when she had fallen asleep.

She longed for James' return so that she might be assured of his continued devotion. If only she could bask in the warmth of his gaze, the curve of his lips when he smiled at her, she would know all was right.

Yet he did not return until late afternoon. The shadows were creeping into the corners of her chamber when Papa knocked upon her door and said, "Mr. Summers has returned. He asked me to tell you that he has found a cottage to let not two miles hence."

Lydia smiled. "That is good news, though I wish he were not going at all. I shall miss having him here in the house."

Geoffrey took the seat Eve had vacated and said, "I wish you would reconsider this attachment. You know how it worries me."

"I suppose you feel as Eve does. You would rather I form an attachment with Reginald."

"I would, as a matter of fact. Though he has no property, at least with him you would not be put into danger."

"You would rather I marry a man I dislike and be miserable the rest of my days? I assure you, I would rather die."

Geoffrey ran his hand over his chin. "Of course I would not want you to choose a man you dislike. If you are happy with James, I shall not say another word. I shall be glad for your happiness and keep my worries to myself."

Lydia reached out to him. "Thank you, Papa. Your sanction means a great deal to me."

He nodded. "Brief as it was, I would not deprive you of what I had with Mariah." He leaned over and kissed her cheek. "James would like to see you. I shall send Sarah in to sit with the two of you."

Sarah knitted unobtrusively in a corner while James sat beside Lydia, eager to tell her all about his find. "It is only a small cottage, but it is not far away.

I shall be able to come and court you every day. You will hardly know that I am not here in the house."

"I wish you were."

He smiled at her, and she felt her heart leap.

He whispered so that Sarah would not hear. "I cannot bear to be away from you, either. That is why I am proposing that we marry. Would you consent to the setting of a date?"

"Nothing could make me happier." Tears of joy filled her eyes. "We shall be happy, shall we not, James? You will not ever tire of me and go off to seek adventure?"

"How could I? I would not be happy without you."

"Eve has assured me that she is far more capable of holding your interest."

"What is there to hold? I have no interest in her at all. You are far more captivating than she could ever hope to be."

She smiled. "That is just what I needed to hear."

"Then I shall tell you every day that you are the most enchanting woman on the face of the earth."

Lydia laughed. "I shall look forward to hearing it. When will Papa and I be invited to see your house?"

"I am moving in on the morrow. If you are feeling quite well in a couple of days, I shall invite the both of you to supper. I found an old shipman in the village to be my cook. He is a bit rough but assures me that he has cooked for an admiral and can make anything I might want."

Lydia cocked her head, her interest piqued "How did you find him so quickly? There was hardly time for an advertisement."

"I had no need of an advertisement. I met him in the pub. He was telling stories in exchange for a drink. When he said that he was in need of employment, I offered him the job."

"So he is new to town?"

"Yes. I am afraid he is a bit of a drifter. Who knows how long he will stay."

Lydia shook her head. "He will probably poison us with his uncivilized cooking."

"Not if he cooked for an admiral."

Lydia gave him an indulgent smile. "And you believe everything you hear? I am afraid you are too trusting."

"Would you rather I had chosen a willing village lass?"

Seeing the teasing light in his eyes, she bit back a smile. "I would have been jealous, you know."

He laughed heartily. "That is what I wanted to hear. We are good for each other, do you not think?"

"I do." Lydia flushed and whispered. "I quite forgot that Sarah is in the room."

"Let her have a bit of gossip to tell the others. It is innocent enough, as we will be married soon," he whispered back. "Now, about that date . . ."

"I was thinking the middle of spring should give me time to make all the arrangements."

"You have already given it thought. I am happy to hear it."

"It is all I shall think about from now on."

His lips curved into a delighted smile. "I doubt it. I know you too well for that. But it pleases me that you are happy to wed me. I never thought to meet such a charming and intriguing creature as you, my Lydia. I cannot believe my fortune."

"Nor can I with you."

He glanced at Sarah, who pretended to be absorbed in her work. He longed to kiss Lydia before he took leave. Yet he knew full well that Sarah was attentive to every gesture and word that passed between them. Thus he curbed his ardor, and, taking Lydia's hand, he pressed it gently and said, "I must go now and begin packing for my move. I shall come to you tomorrow before I leave. You rest tonight and get fully well so that I may show you my cottage."

"I shall, for I am curious. Curious enough to take a chance on your man's cooking."

He laughed. "Perhaps you shall be surprised."

"I hope that I shall be pleasantly surprised."

"So do I. Remember that I must eat it every day."

"Only for a while."

James raised an eyebrow. "Shall we come back to live here in the spring after we are married?"

"I am sure we shall. Papa would not wish for both of us to leave."

He rubbed her fingers. "He does not want to lose

you, and neither do I. He worries about you, Lydia. He fears you will meet your mother's fate."

"I know. But there is nothing to be done for it, for I do not know how to spare him the worry."

"Neither do I. I suppose it was terribly hard for him to see her die and know that he was meant to be in her place."

Lydia nodded. "It has haunted him his whole life. It haunts him still."

"That is too bad. I say, be done with the past, and live in the present."

Lydia smiled. "And I say, bully for you, James Summers."

He released her hand with a gentle squeeze. "I need to let you rest. And I must go finish my packing."

"I shall rise and bid you good-bye before you leave tomorrow."

"Only if you are feeling up to a short time out of bed. And if you are too tired to see me off, you need not worry. I shall come and see you so often, you will not have a chance to miss me."

Lydia's eyes misted with happy tears. "I shall hold you to that promise."

As he bowed out of the room, Lydia wiped the moisture from her cheeks. She looked forward to the day when they did not have to be parted. Yet she supposed, if he were going to court her, it would look better to do so from a separate residence.

Nonetheless, she missed knowing that he was down the hall, only a short distance away should she wish to see him.

The evening dragged by. Lydia took supper in her room, watching the embers of the fire as they cascaded about the grate. Later she read a Jane Austen novel and, though she found it most interesting, had difficulty concentrating on the plot. She kept thinking of James. She marveled that he would still have her, even though she was no more than the daughter of a maid. Certainly theirs was a true love, a love that would last forever. When she finally became drowsy, she slipped beneath her down coverlet and drifted off with a smile upon her face.

The next morning, when James had seen to the loading of his borrowed wagon, he found Lydia waiting for him in the foyer. He wrapped her in a swift embrace and said, "You should not be so near the door. I have let in a draft, and you will be chilled."

She grinned up at him, her expression impish. "I am quite well, sir, and not in the least danger of worsening again."

He kissed her nose. "If you say so."

She drew him toward the parlor. "You have promised to invite us soon."

"As soon as I am settled and the kitchen is sorted out."

"To think, I did not even know you until a few

weeks ago, and now I feel as though we have always been together."

He ran a finger along the curve of her bottom lip. "I feel the very same. And soon we shall always be together." He bent and kissed her gently upon rose lips that would not be denied. "I must go now. The driver is waiting for me, and it is very cold in the wind."

Lydia followed him to the door, where he turned and asked, "Is your father about?"

She shook her head. "I do not believe he is up yet."

He pointed to the silver salver that sat upon the high table beside the door. "I have left a note thanking him for his hospitality. Would you be kind enough to see that he gets it?"

"Certainly. In time, I believe Papa will become very fond of you."

"That would make our lives entirely perfect."

He studied her for a moment, memorizing each detail of her delicate face and the soft dark locks that curled against it. She seemed as fragile as china and transitory as fairy dust. He feared that she would disappear if he let her out of his sight, that he would come back only to find out that she had been a beautiful figment of his imagination.

He shook off the ridiculous notion and, putting his hand upon the doorknob, said, "Scoot upstairs to your fire, or I shall be miserable, worrying about your health."

"I should not ever want to make you miserable."

With a last glance back, Lydia moved to the bottom of the stairs. When she turned around, James was gone. Though she heard the scurrying steps of maids and the clatter of pans, the house seemed strangely empty. It occurred to her that it was her heart that was empty and not the house. And her heart would not be full again until James returned.

She spent a pleasant enough day in the library reading with Papa. All was quiet until a visit by Reginald Smyth in late afternoon. Lydia was just preparing to go upstairs for a rest when Sarah announced his arrival.

"Mr. Smyth to see you, miss."

Sarah rose to greet him as Papa, who was dozing by the fireside, opened his eyes.

Reginald strode into the room.

"Please sit, Mr. Smyth," Lydia invited.

Reginald perched rigidly forward in the matched chair. "I hope what I have heard is not true."

"What have you heard, Mr. Smyth?"

"That you are to wed Mr. James Summers."

"It is true that we have made plans to marry in the spring."

Reginald flared his thin nostrils. "Preposterous, ridiculous. It is not a suitable match at all."

He turned to Papa. "Sir, you must talk some sense into your daughter. You cannot allow her to marry a seaman come from India to claim your estate. How could you trust such a man? He may have acquired many bad habits while at sea. That sort often does."

Geoffrey gave a weary sigh. "I did not think it for the best. But they are determined, and there is no reasoning with Lydia when she has made up her mind."

"You are her father. You must *make* her change her mind."

Lydia exploded from her seat. She faced Reginald. Shaking with fury, she said, "How dare you speak as though I am not even here? It is my future you are challenging, and I believe I should have a say in it. I assure you, I know James well enough, and you have said nothing to change my mind."

Taken aback, Reginald blinked at her. Then, features rigid, he rose to tower above her petite form. Though she took a step back, she did not avert her determined gaze from his face.

He bowed stiffly. "I see that my opinions are unwelcome here. I had hoped to convince you to make a different match, but if you are determined to follow a disastrous course, then you shall have to face the consequences. Do not say that I did not warn you."

Lydia watched his stiff posture, so unyielding, so cold as he walked out of the room. She shuddered. She could never love a man so lacking in passion, so indifferent to the needs of the heart. Always rational, never spontaneous.

Nonetheless, his ominous words left her with a feeling of unease. His warning put her on edge. She tried to put his words out of her mind and tell herself that all would be well. Nothing would upset her plans with James.

Chapter Nine

Lydia awoke after a restless sleep. A glance at the clock told her it was nearly time to dress for supper. Sarah would arrive soon to help her with her hair. She wished James were still in the house. Reginald's words haunted her, and she wished to know that James was well and to draw comfort from his presence. He would make her laugh at her silly fears, her superstitions about the past. For she realized that it was not only Reginald's dire predictions that had upset her, but those from the past, written long ago in the beautiful script of Mariah's hand.

Mariah had lived with the fear of imminent danger. Her death had justified those fears. Lydia did not want to inherit that burden. Yet how could she escape if she married the heir to the estate?

She swung her feet to the floor and slid into pale pink slippers. She squared her shoulders as she padded to the dressing table. As she sat before the mirror, she looked into her steady dark eyes and determined that she would not be afraid of a ghost from the past. Nothing, especially Reginald's jealousy, would keep her from finding happiness with James.

Sarah tapped on her door and asked, "Shall I help you get ready, miss?"

"Do my hair please, Sarah, for I can never get it clasped the way I like, and you have such a talent with hair."

Sarah blushed. "Thank you, miss."

Lydia's smile reflected up at Sarah. "You are invaluable to me. I hope that *you* are not planning to get married and leave me."

Sarah's cheeks flushed. "I shan't, miss. Not just yet anyway." The girl bit her lip and said, "Something has been bothering me, miss. If I may be bold, may I ask you what you think?"

Lydia twisted around to look up at Sarah. "You may ask anything you like."

"Miss Smyth asked about my particular training as a lady's maid, in case she decided to hire me. Were you thinkin' of lettin' me go?"

The girl's worried face made Lydia's temper flare. "Certainly not. But I am sure I can explain it quite easily. Miss Smyth has the intent of rising in her social standing. She is casting about for suitable help when she does so."

Sarah thought it over. "That relieves me. I donna' think I would want to work for her."

"And you shall not have to."

When Sarah finished Lydia's hair, Lydia excused her to finish her evening chores and take supper in the kitchen while she went down to dine with Papa. She walked the length of the mahogany table, decked with silver and white linen, to sit beside him. When their supper had been served and they were alone, she said, "I cannot believe the nerve of Eve and her brother. They are both insufferable, and I wish they had never come to live so near us."

Geoffrey looked mildly surprised. "I know you do not fancy Reginald, but I had believed that you and Eve were friends."

Lydia frowned. "We were friends, of sorts, I suppose. Yet I have always felt that if ever I was a liability in her quest for society, she would easily abandon me."

"And has she abandoned you?"

"Not exactly, though she is furious about my engagement. She had intended to secure James for herself. But that is not why I am angry."

Lydia took a sip of water to calm her escalating fury. Geoffrey studied his daughter as though hesitant to hear the explanation. Nonetheless, he set down his roll and asked, "Why are you angry?"

"Eve has been interviewing our servants behind our backs. She asked Sarah about her training as a lady's maid. She plans to hire them from under us as soon as she can afford to do so. It is very unfair. Good servants are hard to find so far from London."

Geoffrey smiled in obvious relief. "Is that all that is troubling you? I should have thought it a more serious matter to upset you so keenly. You need not worry about the servants. I have enough connections in London to find excellent help, though I doubt we shall lose any. They are treated well and seem quite satisfied."

"It is not that. It is the principle of the matter. Do you not find it presumptuous? Does it not bother you?"

Geoffrey speared a bite of beef. "Not at all. You must not take offense in such minor matters. It was, perhaps, poor judgment, but what could be expected? She has not been fortunate in her circumstance. Perhaps she does not know better."

This comment put an end to the discussion. Taking Geoffrey's implication, Lydia had no right to complain about Eve, for Eve had not been as fortunate as herself. Would her own manners be adequate had she not had the advantage of adoption? Yet it did not stop her from thinking that Eve was cunning and would stop at nothing to achieve the position she envisioned.

Geoffrey fell into his customary silence as he

sipped his wine. As they finished the meal, Lydia's thoughts drifted to a tall, golden-haired man with blue eyes that sparkled when he teased her. She missed his merry banter that never failed to cheer her when her thoughts became dark. He was the missing piece of herself. Without him, she no longer felt whole.

She was jarred from her thoughts when Geoffrey cleared his throat and said, "I have given it some thought, and I should like for you and James to reside here after you are married."

Lydia had hoped he would decide thusly and was thoroughly pleased. "Oh, Papa, nothing could make me happier. I did not want to leave you or Holly Green Manor."

He looked abashed by her enthusiasm. "I felt it must be drafty in that cottage James has let. You would be ill all the time and would only need come here to recover. Why not stay here to start?"

Lydia stifled a grin. "Indeed, you are right. We would save a great deal of trouble by residing at Holly Green. I cannot imagine that anywhere else would be as comfortable or conducive to health."

"Indeed, though, you must have a honeymoon. Where shall you go?"

Lydia felt like giggling. "I have not given it a thought."

"Your mother and I went to Bath. It is lovely in the spring."

"I shall talk to James. Perhaps we might go to Bath."

Geoffrey's expression took on a faraway look. "We stayed at the Royal Crescent, Mariah and I. We rented a house for the spring, attended plays at the Theatre Royale, and soaked in the Roman baths. We took long walks to see the gardens. They are lovely in the spring."

The bittersweetness of his reminiscence softened the rigid lines of his thin face, allowing Lydia to see a resemblance to the portrait of the young man he had once been. She had often stared at the painting and wondered at the change from the handsome young man with deep blue eyes and a mischievous grin to the solemn-faced man she called Papa.

The portrait reminded her a great deal of James, for there was a strong family resemblance. He had the same blue eyes and mischievous grin. Had Geoffrey once also had a carefree and adventurous spirit? The thought struck her as strange. She had never been able to imagine Geoffrey other than the way she had known him when she was a little girl. By then, the burden of Mariah's death had weighed heavily upon him.

In those few moments of contemplation, sympathy blossomed for him. She had never experienced such tragedy in her own life. If she had, perhaps she would have been as silent and aloof as Geoffrey had been with her. For years she had faulted him. Yet how would she behave if she were suddenly left without James?

She shivered as she shook the dark thought aside. Nothing was going to happen to James. There would be no tragedies. They were all healthy and well and would stay so for years. She must not let herself dwell on the past, though it did give her a new appreciation for what Papa had been through.

She started when he said, "You have gone very quiet. Did I say something to upset you?"

She shook her head and smiled. "No, not at all. I loved hearing about your trip to Bath. I can imagine both of you, from your portraits, young and carefree, strolling the streets."

"The circus was Mariah's favorite. She loved going there to pop into shops and see the peddlers and the acrobats in the streets. And she loved the flowers that were abloom. She always loved flowers, especially roses. I have tried to see to our roses all these years just because she loved them so."

Lydia cocked her head. "That is interesting to me. I always thought that you had a passion for roses. But it was for the sake of Mama."

He nodded. "My interests lie in the areas of business and investments. Horses, too. I remember when I purchased your mare. Fine deal, if I say so myself."

"She is a fine horse, and I love her dearly. Though we are not truly related, I suppose I share your passion for horses."

"We are related. The bond of time has made us so."

He studied her. "Mariah would be proud of you. You have grown to be a fine, levelheaded young woman. Though I should have said it sooner, I want you to know that I am proud of you too. Until you came home, I never spent enough time with you to realize it."

Lydia's eyes filled with tears. "Thank you, Papa. You will always be my true father."

He cleared his throat. "Yes, well, I suppose we had best retire to the drawing room. The servants will be waiting to clear up supper."

They had barely stood to leave when a kitchen maid appeared, ready to clear the sideboard. Lydia knew that the girl must be eager to finish up her work and retire for the evening, for she would feel the same if she were in her place.

Lydia preceded Geoffrey to the drawing room, where he took out his beloved papers to study all the financial news from London, while Lydia took up her book to finish the last chapter. Before she reached the end of the book, she found herself staring into the fire, wondering if James were thinking of her as she was of him. How wonderful a life they would have. Soon they would be man and wife and would not have to spend their evenings apart. He would be right back in this house again, sitting with her as they read beside the fire. And when it was time to retire, she would not have to go up alone to a cold bed-chamber. She smiled at the thought of awakening to his smile every morning. How bright it would make each day.

And Papa? He would learn to treasure having his nephew about. He would have someone with whom to ride and hunt and talk about the business news of the world. The three of them would become a real family, and, one day, when there were children, there would be their chatter and companionship to keep Papa amused.

It grew late as Lydia mused. The fire died down, and when, at last, Geoffrey proposed that they each go to bed, Lydia drew herself reluctantly from her cozy niche upon the settee and plodded up to her chambers. She slipped into a checked cotton gown before settling at her dressing table to brush out her hair.

When she finished, Sarah brought a warmed brick for her feet, and Lydia padded across her thick rug to hop into bed. She slid beneath the covers and settled her icy feet against the wrapping on the brick.

When Sarah had bid her good night and left the room, Lydia blew out her candle and snuggled into her blankets. As the warmth from the brick seeped into her bones, she thought of how contented she was with life. She was closer to Papa than she had ever thought possible. And James had promised to ride over every day to see her. These comforting thoughts settled in her mind and lulled her to sleep.

She arose early the next morning and dined downstairs in the breakfast room. Surrounded by windows, she was well able to assess the weather. Fleecy white clouds filled the sky. The trees were still, and there was no sign of rain. Perhaps she might talk James into taking a ride.

She finished breakfast and went upstairs to dress in her blue velvet riding habit. She brushed her hair into silky waves and donned her matching blue cap. She smoothed her skirt and adjusted her coat before appraising her appearance in her full-length mirror. Assured that she looked her best, she scurried down the stairs in hopes that James would arrive soon.

Papa had not yet arisen. The only indications that there were others in the house were the muted sounds of servants going about their chores—the clatter of a dish in the kitchen, Sarah singing softly as she dusted the parlor. Lydia informed the butler that she would be in the library, should any guests arrive. The good man raised a dark eyebrow at the possibility of any such early arrivals, replied that he would be happy to direct them to the library, and went about his task of counting the silver.

James finished the breakfast that Grayson had made. He was relieved to have found someone who made no complaints regarding the rustic kitchen, which consisted of a fireplace and hob for hanging a pot. He had to admit that he cooked well for a haggard old seaman. His plain and simple fare of sausage, biscuits, and eggs had been tasty, especially after James worked up an appetite by spending the early-morning hours taking stock of his rental and its surroundings.

He had begun by a walk down the weedy path to the henhouse. Any hope he harbored of raising hens was dashed when he saw the condition of the shelter. Splintered red boards stood sentinel around a sod roof that had long since caved in. The low stone fence about the yard had crumbled, thus allowing entrance to any fox that had a mind to steal a chicken. Indeed, a putrid stench suggested that other creatures had often inhabited the deserted structure.

The stone barn was solid but needed a good cleaning and fresh straw. He would see to the purchase of hay and straw when he rode out to see Lydia. Surely one of Geoffrey's tenants would be happy to sell some.

The cottage gardens were overgrown and needed tending. But if luck continued to smile upon him, he would not be here long enough into spring to worry about them. He would reside with Lydia in the home that he would inherit, the home that would be in their family for many generations to come.

He smiled as he thought of Lydia and their future

together. They would tend their manor and be good stewards of their tenants. How fine it would be to own a home of his own. He had never owned anything except his horse. In India, he had lived in an Army home with his father, and then lived aboard ship until he came back to England. He had rented in London, and he rented now.

He had only to win Geoffrey's favor for all to be truly perfect. He hoped it would be a comfort to the gentleman to have someone to care for his estate in his declining years, someone who cared about it as he did, and someone who would love and care for his daughter when he could no longer do so.

As he walked out to saddle his horse, he felt cheerfully optimistic about winning over the lord of the manor. Once Geoffrey saw how happy they all were, he could have no objections to their marriage. Indeed, like a fairy-tale ending, he intended for each of them to live happily ever after.

He saddled up and rode from the stable. In a short while he would be with Lydia. He wondered if she had been thinking of him, anticipating his arrival as eagerly as he longed for her. It seemed like much more than a day since he had last seen her. Each time they were parted, he worried that she might change her mind. He needed assurance that she truly had agreed to become his wife and would not go back on her pledge. For to ever live in that house without her would be torture. He would imagine her next to him each time he sat in front of the library hearth. He would see her face smiling at him across the dining table, and he would ride alone across the meadow and wish that she were cantering beside him on her little mare. The house, without Lydia, could never be more than an empty shell. With her, it would be a beloved home.

He nudged his horse into a trot as he headed for the road. It was a perfect day for a ride. The sky was fair with white dumpling clouds. The chill in the air invigorated his senses. High in the sky a falcon circled, hunting a rabbit or field mouse. He admired the magnificence of the bird of prey. It was strong and sure, determined and swift, a deadly hunter that never hunted for sport but only to fulfill its needs.

He hummed a tune as he rode along, enjoying the warmth of the sunshine as it broke through the clouds. A few miles farther he reached the winding lane that led to Lydia's house. He winced as he remembered the first time he had laid eyes on her. She had pressed herself against the hedge to keep from being crushed by his coach. Since that ill-begun meeting, their lives had grown entwined. He doubted there was a couple more devoted to each other in the entire county.

He could not wait to be alone with her. He felt sure she would consent to join him on a ride when he arrived. With her penchant for riding, she was sure to think it a splendid idea. He was so engrossed in his pleasant thoughts that the bullet took him quite by surprise. It sped past his ear so fast that he felt the rush of air as it passed.

Stunned, he reined his horse and looked about. Not believing himself in danger, he thought a stray bullet must have crossed his path. And yet his instinct for caution, formed from years of military service, urged him to be prudent. If he continued to sit and scan the copse of trees that lay beyond the grassy meadow, he was choosing to be an easy target. He pulled about. Nudging the horse, they splayed gravel as they headed full tilt toward the manor.

Another bullet passed behind him, making it hard to believe they were stray shots. Someone was aiming at him intentionally. And he would be lucky to reach the manor alive. Yet speed was on his side. He had a fast horse, and since it was difficult to hit a moving target, he reached the manor lawn without harm. He dismounted as soon as he reined to a halt and left the horse to await a groom.

Bounding forward, he rang the front bell. The butler opened the door with customary formality. He uttered a startled grunt as James barreled past him, relieved to have reached the safety of the foyer.

"Close the door, man. There is a mad person outside."

The butler drew his black eyebrows into a puzzled frown. "I beg your pardon, sir."

"Beg whatever you like, but close the door. Someone is shooting at me."

With a startled, "Oh, my," the man hastened to close the door.

"Where is Miss Summers? She is not outside, is she?"

"I believe she is in the library, sir."

James turned about, leaving the servant to stare after him. He hurried along the hall and burst into the library. He would not be satisfied until he could see, with his own eyes, that she was safe.

She rose when he burst into the room. The bright smile that lit her face faded as she saw his intense expression. She stepped forward, reaching her hands to him.

"James, what is it? Whatever is the matter?"

"I was shot at on the way down the lane."

Her face drained of color. "Are you sure? Perhaps it was a hunter out shooting for game. I could ask Papa if he has given permission."

"There was no game where I was riding. I was quite out in the open when two shots came very near my head."

Lydia sank into a chair beside the library door. "Then it is happening, just as I feared it would. Now that you have returned, someone is trying to kill you. It is the curse."

"It is no such thing," James protested, though he

felt less sure than he sounded. For what reason could any of his neighbors have for wishing him dead?

"Then what?" she asked.

"I have no idea. Perhaps I was mistaken for someone else."

Lydia fidgeted with the lace on her kerchief. "I suppose that is possible. And yet I cannot think of anyone else whose death would benefit another."

"No angry tenants? Someone with a grudge?"

She shook her head. "We have always got along well with our tenants."

James nodded. "I thought as much."

She stood and looked up into his face. "This means you must be very careful. You must not take chances. You must stay here in the house."

James gave her a rueful smile. "For the rest of my life? You know I could not be happy hiding in a house. Instead, I will find out who is at the bottom of this."

"And how will you do that?" Lydia felt her heart beating rapidly with alarm. The last thing she wanted to hear was that James planned to go about seeking out his would-be killer. He would surely be killed, and they would never be married. A life without him was more than she could bear.

Before he could answer, she said, "You must do no such thing. You are at a terrible disadvantage. While you do not know who is trying to kill you, they do know you. You will sacrifice your life, and no one will be able to prove who has done it. And then the killer will live right here in this house."

She sank back into the chair and began to sob. James looked on, feeling helpless to stem her tears. He could not solve the mystery of his assailant while hiding in the house. He squatted and placed his hands gently upon her shoulders.

"Lydia, listen to me. If this man wants to kill me, it will do no good to hide. He will seek me right here in the house. Remember how your mother was killed in her own attic?"

Lydia nodded. She had to admit the truth in his observation. As long as someone was out there and unknown, he would not be safe. Still, if he were determined to seek his assailant's identity, she was determined to do no less. And she already had a suspect in mind.

Chapter Ten

"Perhaps I shall hire a detective," James mused aloud.

He sat next to Lydia upon the settee and held her hand as he spoke.

"It might take some time to retain one," Lydia said.

"How else do you propose I get to the bottom of this? If I go poking my nose into bushes, I am likely to get shot."

"I do not think you should poke about the bushes. I agree you should let others delve into the matter instead. Perhaps I might find a way to lure the assassin into the open."

James rubbed his hand down his chin. "Yes. I like the idea of setting a trap. However, I want you to stay entirely clear of it. I will not take chances with your safety."

Lydia nodded dutifully, all the while knowing precisely what she was going to do. And since she was firmly set upon her course of action, there was no point in discussing it with James. He would forbid her to leave the house. And he would tell Papa. And Papa would also tell her not to leave the house. So she would tell neither of them and do as she pleased.

When Geoffrey joined them, he was so disturbed by news of the shooting that he sank into a chair and fortified himself with a stiff glass of brandy. He shook his head and said, "It is exactly what I feared. You are a magnet for danger, Mr. Summers, just as I was so many years ago. What will you do about it? You cannot remain here and put Lydia in danger."

"Papa," Lydia protested. "Would you have us turn him out onto the road? Whoever shot at him might still be out there. How would you live with your conscience if Mr. Summers were shot?"

Geoffrey sighed deeply and took a long swallow of his liquor. It seemed to steady his nerves, if not his hands, and he said, "You are right. Mr. Summers may stay until after supper and then slip away in the dark."

James nodded. "My plan exactly."

Lydia shifted in her chair to face them both with a frown. "If the assailant believes him to be in this house, I fail to see how it will help us if he slips away."

"It will help him if his attacker comes looking here for him," Geoffrey said.

Lydia thought over the logic and admitted, "That is true, if he can get away without being seen."

She turned to James. "I would not be able to sleep all night for worry that you did not make it home. And yet, if it is truly safer . . ."

James patted her hand. "I shall be fine. I can move very quietly when the need calls for it."

Lydia nodded. "Then I suppose you must go. But not until after supper. And we must create a diversion so that anyone watching will be drawn away from you."

James smiled. "What do you have in mind?"

"We shall send for the coach to be brought 'round to the front of the house. Tom the coachman will wait there for a time so that it will seem we are planning to go out. You may make your escape from the stables while all attention is upon the coach."

James raised his eyebrows. "I am impressed. You have quite the mind for intrigue. It is a good plan. Do you not think so, Uncle?"

Geoffrey nodded. "A very good plan. Of course, Lydia will not go near the coach."

"Of course not," James agreed. "I shall stay until after supper and then make my escape. I will send my man, Grayson, over in the morning to assure Miss Lydia of my safe return."

Lydia shuddered. "The wait will be interminable. I shall ride over in the morning to check on you myself."

Geoffrey shook his head. "Oh, I do not like that at all. Whoever is out there may not be too particular about his target."

James' regretful smile pierced Lydia's heart. "You will only worry your father. Let my man come. I will think of a way to see you soon."

Lydia sighed, unable to think of an argument. "As you wish."

They sat together in the library and then took a stroll through the wide gallery that led to the parlor. They stopped at each portrait, and Lydia named the ones that James could not.

"It is odd, that I, who am unrelated to the family, should know more about their heritage than you, a blood relation," Lydia remarked.

"It is hard to keep up with relations when one resides so far away as India."

She nodded. "I am sure that it is."

He placed his arm around her waist as they perused the paintings. "We will be here, one day, immortalized for all posterity."

Lydia shuddered. "I cannot imagine sitting for a portrait. It must be dreadfully tedious."

James laughed. "I am not surprised that *you* feel that way. Most women are vain enough to put up with the boredom, but you do not find it at all tempting."

"Indeed, I do not. Are you sure it must be done?"

He shook his head, feigning a serious expression. "I am afraid so. As you see, it is a family tradition."

She reached up to run her fingers along his cheek. "Then I shall endure it just for you."

Later in the afternoon, she found it hard to tear herself away from him when she excused herself to her room, ostensibly for a rest before supper. James went off to join Geoffrey in the drawing room to offer him a rolled cheroot.

Her hands shook as she changed into her riding costume. She felt a keen disgust for the man who made this errand necessary, for their parting had not been pleasant, and she had no desire to see him again. Yet, for James, she would do anything, even this.

She tied the ribands of her bonnet and slipped quietly from her room. She was relieved to discover no maids in the hall, no one to see her depart. She slipped down the back stairs and eased out the door that led outside. She made haste to the stables. Once arrived, she glanced behind her and was assured that she had escaped unseen.

The sky had turned iron gray. She bit back dismay at the thought of snow. Surely the weather would hold until she completed her errand.

She found the young stable boy and beckoned him to her. In a whisper she told him, "Saddle two horses, and tell the hostler that I am sending you on an errand. Do not tell him I am going with you. Bring the horses out when he is not looking."

The boy gave her a curious look but raised no question. He found the old hostler in a far stall and repeated what he was told to say. A few moments later the lad returned.

"He said to hurry. It looks like a good snow is coming."

Lydia glanced out the open stable door into the gray gloom of late afternoon. "He may be right. Bring the horses right away."

The boy assisted her onto her horse, and when he was also mounted, she said, "We are not going far. Follow me."

She turned her horse away from the shelter of the stable and felt the bite of the wind upon her cheeks and nose. A snowflake drifted down upon her lashes as she pressed her horse into a canter. The boy followed, keeping a proper horse length behind her.

They slowed as they turned onto the rutted lane that led to the Smyth cottage. It looked drab and forbidding in the fading light. The only sign of welcome was a pale trail of smoke that curled from the chimney. Lydia had only called once before, not long after Eve moved in. Eve had seemed so embarrassed with her abode and spoke so fondly of the fashionable home they had left in London that Lydia had decided to let Eve pay calls upon her instead.

And now, Lydia thought with a scowl, if she were right about Reginald, Eve might soon find herself alone in the world. She should have suspected sooner. Reginald's cold eyes should have given him away. It made so much sense now that she could not ignore her suspicions. Yet she knew both Papa and James would think her silly to jump to this conclusion.

As they walked the horses to the front of the house, Lydia noted that no one had bothered to fix the shutter that hung loose from the wall or to paint the shabby oak door. Perhaps it was because the Smyths did not plan to live here long. And one way out of their circumstances would be Reginald's marriage to her.

The boy, Tom, helped her from her mare and took the two horses away to what passed for a stable. She knew he would see to their comfort before his own. She must remember to see to it that he got something warm to drink when they arrived home again.

She hit the ancient brass ring that served as knocker soundly against the door. After a moment she heard footsteps. Reginald pulled open the door. A flicker of surprise passed over his hawklike features when he saw Lydia standing upon his stoop.

He blinked several times as though to assure himself that he was not imagining her presence. Then, assured that she was not merely a vision, he said,

"Why, Lydia, whatever brings you out in this impending storm? You must come inside, or you will freeze. I will tell Eve you are here."

He stepped aside, and Lydia said, "I have every intention of coming inside. And it is you I have come to see."

The force of her declaration caused him to raise his eyebrows. "Me? You made it perfectly clear you did not wish to have anything to do with me."

She inclined her head to look up at him. "Nor have I changed my mind."

He gestured to the small parlor that lay to the left of the door. "Please come and sit. I am intrigued with regard to what is on your mind."

Lydia settled upon a rather shabby, stiff-backed chair upholstered in blue velvet. Reginald settled upon its twin.

She took a deep breath to calm her agitation. Before she could speak, Eve appeared in the doorway, wearing a worn cotton dress and a faded paisley shawl. She pulled the shawl more tightly around her when she saw Lydia.

"Well, look who is here. Do you not think yourself too good to be seen with us?"

Lydia lost her train of thought as she tried to understand Eve's comment. She could only conceive that Eve was annoyed because Lydia had turned down Reginald's hand in marriage.

"If you are referring to—"

Eve interrupted. "I shall have you know that we are every bit as much gentry as you—more so, if truth were known."

It was obvious that she would have gone on except for the fact that Reginald held up a hand to stop her. "Please, Eve. I do wonder as to the purpose of Miss Summers' visit. I shall not have my curiosity assuaged if you continue upon this track."

He fixed his scrutiny upon Lydia, and she felt her muscles tense with renewed anger. "I shall very gladly tell you the reason for my visit. You believe that if you kill James, I shall be forced to marry you. I am here to tell you that your effort to that end has had quite the opposite effect. I would not marry you even if you were successful. Instead, I should expend every effort to prove your guilt and see that you were hanged."

Even though the house was chilly, Lydia felt flushed with the heat of her emotions. If he dared harm James, she was bound to see that justice was done. Her heart pounded with the strength of her determination to make him see that she would carry out her threat. And now that he knew her feelings on the matter, she hoped to convince him to abandon his plan.

He fixed her with a cold stare. "Are you implying, madam, that I have endeavored to slay Mr. Summers?"

Lydia ignored Eve's gasp as she met Reginald's

gaze. "I cannot think of anyone else who would have a reason to kill him."

"And you think I would risk hanging just to marry you?"

"With no one left to inherit, I could believe you would risk much to have a living from the estate."

"Then you are foolish as well as vain. I do not fancy you enough to commit murder or to hang for you."

His eyes were steely, his voice as cold as granite. Not a hint of guilt rested upon his features.

Lydia shivered. He looked as though he meant every word he said. Had she been mistaken?

Eve recovered her senses and said, "You are indeed Miss High and Haughty. You treated my brother abominably, and now you have the nerve to come here and say these horrible things?"

Lydia caught her lower lip between her teeth. She had expected that Reginald might deny his wrongful action, yet she was unprepared for such a convincing denial from both of them.

"If I was mistaken, I owe each of you an apology. Yet, I want you to know that I shall be diligent in my search for whoever shot at James."

"That is understandable. But you will not find him here," Reginald said.

Lydia rose from her seat. "I must be going back. I want to return before supper."

Eve leaned forward. "Since you have apologized,

I must insist that you have a quick cup of tea with me in my room. It will warm you for your journey."

Lydia nodded. "I accept. And if it is not too much trouble, could you have your kitchen maid make a cup for my groom? He has been outside with the horses, and I am sure he is nearly frozen."

"I shall take care of it right away. Come up to my room and wait."

Lydia took her leave from Reginald, sorry for the ill feeling that lay between them yet still unwilling to risk James' life to keep neighborly peace. She followed Eve up wooden stairs that creaked underfoot to the small chamber that served as her bedroom.

"Go in and make yourself comfortable."

The room was drafty and sported only one small fireplace that had burned low of coal. Lydia shivered, even though she was still clad in her riding jacket. She walked to the window and was dismayed to see the flakes falling steadily from a sky heavy with snow.

"You should stay the night," Eve said.

Lydia turned to her. "It is not far to go home. I should not tarry long, though."

Eve nodded. "Then I shall get our tea, and we can have a very short soiree."

She turned and closed the door swiftly. Lydia heard a key turn in the lock.

She stared at the door, puzzled as to why Eve had locked it. Then she rushed forward and knocked upon it briskly. "Eve, what are you doing? Why have you locked this door?"

"You are my friend," Eve answered cheerfully. "I should not want you to perish in the snow. Since I know you will not listen to reason, I have no choice except to lock you inside."

"Papa and James will worry when my groom tells them I did not return."

"La, you are not of so much more import than your groom. He must stay too. I would not have his death on my conscience. I will tell your groom that it is your wish that you both remain."

"James will come for me."

"Does he know where you have gone?"

Lydia felt her stomach lurch with the terrible realization that he did not. What if worry drove him to search for her long into the night? He would not know to come here. Their tracks would be covered with snow. And James might freeze from his efforts.

"Please," she begged. "You must let me out. I fear for James if he goes out in the dark searching."

Still cheerful, Eve answered, "Dear Lydia, it is for your own good."

She heard the stairs creak as Eve walked back down. She began to bang upon the door. Perhaps Reginald would see the danger in keeping her here with no message sent home. She banged until her knuckles bled, yet no one came to release her.

She spun about and hurried to the window. Perhaps

it might provide a way down. She had climbed often as a child and had no fear of trying it now. All she needed was a foothold.

She slid open the window and peered down. The wall descended in a straight, sheer line. There was nothing to cling to or break her fall. She clenched her hands, feeling truly desperate.

She saw Tom heading toward the house. Eve must have told him to come to the kitchen for his spot of tea. Lydia leaned out the window and shouted to him. He stared up with a look of surprise.

She motioned for him to stand beneath her. "I am prisoner in this room. You must come and release me. Do not let either Miss Smyth or her brother see you come up the stairs."

When he continued to stare at her, his face screwed up in puzzlement, she said, "They mean to keep us here tonight. We must not stay. Papa and Mr. James will worry."

Tom nodded. He answered conspiratorially, "You can count on me. I will be up directly, Miss Lydia."

Lydia shut the window, feeling a renewed sense of hope. If only Tom could release her, they might slip out and arrive home none the worse for the trip. While she waited for the key to turn in the lock, she glanced about the room. A book lay upon the dressing table, a book that looked so familiar that Lydia stepped over to get a closer look.

She gasped as she spied the cover. It was none

other than the family Bible that had gone missing from the table beside the front door. To be sure, she flipped open the cover and glanced at the familiar family tree that stopped with her father and mother on that line and included James on another. It did not include her name for the simple reason that she was not a true descendant.

Lydia frowned as she closed the Bible. Why did Eve have it on her dressing table? It was obvious that she must have stolen it one day when she left the house. What possible meaning could it have for her?

Her thoughts were distracted as she heard a fumbling at the door. She clasped the Bible to her chest and felt her heart rise to her throat as she prayed that it was Tom who had made his way up to her. She hoped no one else was about. She did not want to think what Reginald would do if he discovered a groom creeping about his house.

Fortunately, Tom edged open the door and glanced timidly inside. "Miss Summers, are you here?"

Lydia hurried to ease past him. She asked in a whisper, "Did you see anyone about when you came up?"

"No, miss. But I heard voices in the kitchen."

"We had best hurry. They may decide to bring up a tray of food."

Lydia held the Bible close as they crept down the stairs, hardly daring to breathe. When they reached the bottom, they paused to listen. All was quiet in the parlor and hall. Silent as mice, they tiptoed around the corner and through the hall. They reached the door and slipped out into the thick white flakes. Their footprints left a clear trail across the porch and onto the lawn. Yet soon it would not matter, if they could not reach the horses and make an escape.

Lydia sped across the powdery lawn and turned the corner of the house. The small stable lay just ahead, close enough to catch the scent of horseflesh in the damp, chilly air. She felt comforted to know that her little mare stood just inside. She would feel even better once they were safely on their way.

Lydia winced at the groan of the wood as Tom pulled open the stable door. Here, in the snow-muted outdoors, every sound seemed magnified by the absence of any other. She only hoped that the clatter of supper preparations within the house would cover any noise they made in escape.

Tom saddled their horses quickly and led them as they left the stable. She could not wait to mount up and start home. She cleared the end of the stable door and gave a gasp of horror as she collided full force into Reginald as he carried a stack of firewood past the door.

She shrank back with a cry of alarm, ignoring the pain where her shoulder hit the wood. She stared at Reginald, watching his scowl of irritation with growing foreboding. He juggled the wood to keep it from falling and then turned his attention to Lydia.

"You are leaving?"

Her disappointment was so keen that she knew she would fight him should he try to stop her. She shook fiercely from agitation and from the cold that was seeping into her bones.

"Do not try to stop me," she warned.

Reginald gave her a keen look. "Why should I stop you? Do you believe I would murder *you* too?"

Lydia felt her blood chill. Could he do such a thing? She really was not sure.

When he continued to block her path, she grabbed a riding crop and said, "Move aside, and let us pass."

A half smile twitched at the corners of his lips. "My, you are a delectable bundle of fury. How I would have relished taming you."

"You will not get a chance. Now, move out of our way."

A flicker of warning in his eyes made her heart pound with the fear that she had taken the wrong approach. Yet he merely stared hard at her and then turned away. "If you are set upon returning, you should go before the storm worsens."

Without a look back, he plowed through the deepening snow toward the house, balancing the heavy bundle in his arms. Lydia stared after him, weak with relief at being released and wondering if he had even known that Eve had held her prisoner. What a strange pair they made.

Tom helped her mount, and they set off toward

the road. Though he said nothing, she could tell by the boy's tense face that he would not be at ease until they reached the safety of Holly Green Manor. She shared his feelings as she urged the horses along as swiftly as possible in their trek through the snow.

By the time they neared the manor, Lydia's fear had faded, leaving in its place outrage at Eve's audacity. Eve coveted power and position. The weather had been no more than a convenient excuse to keep Lydia at her mercy. How she must have relished turning the key that had turned Lydia into a powerless prisoner. And how livid she must be now that her captive had flown. It gave Lydia satisfaction to have thwarted Eve's lust for control. And it stirred her anger to think of how the thoughtless girl could have put James in danger. When they next met, she felt sure that Eve would laugh about it as though it were a joke. Yet it was no joke to Lydia.

She accompanied Tom to the rear of the house before dismounting. He led the horses to the stable, while she slipped inside through the back door. The maids were busy in the kitchen. She met no one as she stole up the stairs. She was just ready to congratulate herself upon her narrow escape when she realized that Papa stood outside his chambers, frowning as he watched her approach.

Chapter Eleven

Geoffrey turned to face her. The pale candlelight in the hallway cast his face in a ghostly pallor. "You were not thinking of taking a ride?"

Lydia shook her head. "No. I discovered that it is snowing."

He eyed her suspiciously. "You know that it is growing dark. Where were you thinking of going?"

"Only for a short ride. This business with James has left me unsettled."

He looked as though he did not wholly believe her. Fortunately, he was distracted by the book she held clasped in her arms.

"Where did you find the family Bible?"

Lydia glanced down. She had quite forgotten she was holding it.

"Eve returned it to me. It seemed she borrowed it and forgot to tell me."

Geoffrey's brows puckered. "How odd. What could she want with it?"

"I have no idea." Lydia was glad she could answer at least that much with honesty.

Geoffrey nodded. "I am sure it was an oversight. Now, you had best dress for supper. I was just going down."

Lydia nodded, hoping Geoffrey did not notice how she shivered. She slipped into her room, thankful that Sarah had the fire blazing on the grate. She changed out of her damp clothing and dressed hurriedly in a warm muslin of pale green.

Sarah knocked at the door a few moments later, and Lydia was thankful to give over the styling of her hair. Her fingers, numb from the cold, were little use in fashioning and smoothing her hair. Sarah's small hands moved with competent ease, pulling the rich brown tresses into a topknot while leaving two tendrils to dangle enticingly from her temples.

Sarah stepped back and viewed her completed work in the dressing-table mirror. "You look lovely, miss."

"Thank you, Sarah."

She did not feel lovely. She felt tired and cold and hungry. She hoped that James did not notice, for he would surely not approve of her outing. For this reason, she would not mention it to him. In fact, she wanted only to put it behind her. Yet the whole outcome still had her puzzled. If Reginald was not the assailant, then who had fired at James?

She went downstairs to join the men. She found them engaged in a friendly exchange of politics as they awaited her. She took James' arm, and they went into the dining room together.

Lydia found that she felt much better after a hearty meal of pork roast and hot puddings. The wine warmed her to her toes, and she began to relax. Even her confrontation with Reginald did not seem as unnerving. For what did Reginald matter when she had James sitting safely at her table and sure not to venture out on such a night as this? They could spend a cozy evening nestled near the fire. Perhaps he might read more poetry to her. They would be cozy in their library with its heavy furniture and comforting scent of old leather volumes, a scent she had loved since childhood.

The gentlemen were agreeable to her suggestion that James stay the night. The deepening snow and falling flakes would make travel hazardous. Nonetheless, James still worried that his presence might put them in danger. To Lydia's surprise, Geoffrey dismissed these fears with a wave of his hand.

"Who would go out on such a frigid night? I believe we will be safe until it clears and you are able to depart."

With that assurance, James settled comfortably

beside Lydia on the upholstered settee whose carved legs had always reminded Lydia of great curved seashells. She leaned onto his shoulder, savoring the warmth of his body. And when he took up the book of poetry and began to read, the low resonance of his voice sent a shiver down her spine.

They stayed thus until the late hours of the night, when James stole a kiss before they retired to their own chambers. Lydia missed the cozy warmth they had shared as she shivered beneath her heavy covers. She drifted to sleep with the image of his clear blue eyes and his rakish blond hair that fell endearingly across his forehead. Each time she roused from sleep, she smiled to herself, comforted by the thought that he was nearby. And when the mid-morning light crept through a crack in her heavy velvet drapes, she opened her eyes and looked forward to having breakfast with him.

She rang for Sarah to help her dress, for she was in a hurry to see James. She donned a deep blue muslin that brought out the darkness of her eyes. She fidgeted as Sarah brushed her hair until it was glossy and then caught up the sides in a clasp that left the rest of the dark, wavy mass to cascade down her back.

Then, feeling as pale as the snow, she bit her lips and pinched her cheeks to bring color to her face. At last satisfied with her appearance, she flew down the stairs like a graceful dove, hoping to find James awaiting her in the breakfast room. She reached the doorway and smiled to see both of her men engrossed in an issue of the London paper.

James rose to his feet, a smile of approval lighting his handsome features. Lydia's heart skipped a beat as she realized how fortunate she was to have fallen in love with such a handsome man and to have him love her in return. Tall and slim, he had the well-muscled grace of a lion. His movements were rarely hurried, yet he possessed in his bearing the aura of reserved power. It was exciting to Lydia simply to watch him cross a room.

Before she could greet either of them, a commotion in the front hallway drew everyone's attention. James rushed past Lydia, saying, "Stay here until we know if something is amiss."

Papa followed, and Lydia followed him, quite unable to stay behind and remain ignorant of what was causing the stir. She peeked out from behind the men to see the old sailor James had hired. He was cursing at the butler and demanding that the stalwart servant let him pass.

James stepped forward and took his arm. "It is all right, Giles. Let him in. I need to know what is wrong."

The old sailor stepped forward. "I shall tell you, sir. Someone has burned down your house, that is what."

James' face drained of color. He took Grayson by

the arm and led him toward the parlor. "Come in, man, and tell me how this happened."

James led Grayson to a chair and then sat facing him. "How bad is the damage?"

Grayson shook his grizzled head. "Terrible. Almost everything is gone. I managed to escape with the clothes on me back and little else. The entire upstairs is gone. Had you been sleepin' there, you would have died, no doubt."

Lydia shivered and sent a prayer of thanks that James had been forced to stay the night. Still, the news of the fire left her with a terrible sense of foreboding. First he had been shot at, and now his house had burned. Surely two such calamities were not random accidents.

As though reading her mind, James asked, "Did you leave a candle burning, perhaps?"

Grayson frowned and swore adamantly, "It was nothing I done, and I swear to that. I left nothin' to burn when I went to bed."

James' nod was resigned. "I believe you. It is good that you managed to escape."

"I never would have waked if not for that ol' tabby what's been hanging 'round. She got scared and jumped on me, mewing and pawing me chest. By then, most of the house was aflame. Smoke was filling the room, so I climbed out the window with the cat."

James sighed. "This is bad news. We have no lodging and no explanation for the fire."

"One thing's odd," Grayson said.

"What is that?"

"The cat ran off for the woods. When I looked to see where she was going, I thought I saw a rider, sitting stone still near the trees, watching the fire. It was too dark to be sure."

Lydia's heart lurched. "Then for sure this was no accident. It was another deliberate attempt to kill you, James." She wrung her hands, feeling helpless. "What shall we do?"

James' jaw went rigid with determination. "Since I have lost everything, I shall go to London to replace my clothing and personal possessions. Then I shall rent another house and discover who is to blame for these assaults."

Geoffrey spoke up for the first time. "I am glad it was not this house that was set afire. Do you see how marriage to Lydia will put her in danger?"

"I agree with you, sir. I intend to keep to myself until this mystery is unraveled. I have no intention of bringing disaster upon this manor or anyone in it. I shall leave this morning for London and take Grayson with me. I will stop at the village pub to put out the word that I shall be gone."

Geoffrey nodded. "A good idea."

"It is not a good idea," Lydia protested. "You

shall be on the road, where you might be accosted."

"We shall be well armed and, with any luck, gone before my assailant knows I have left." He smiled ruefully. "We have little enough to pack."

"How long will you be in London?" Lydia asked.

"Only a fortnight or two. Long enough to refurbish my wardrobe and make inquiries as to other lodgings for let."

Geoffrey sighed. "It is a terrible business, this greed for the manor."

He rang the bell and ordered a round of sherry for each of them. "We shall need our spirits stiffened before facing this day," he said.

They downed the sherry, and Grayson went to the kitchen to take his meal while the rest of the party returned to the breakfast room. A glance at Lydia, who was unusually pensive, made James wonder where her thoughts were leading her. She could be rash, and if she had concocted some plan to catch the guilty party before he returned, he wanted to know of it.

As she toyed with her poached egg, he asked, "Are you scheming to solve this before I return?"

She glanced up, taking great pains to look innocent. "I am not, though I have been thinking that it might be best if you remain in London for a while. You are safer where your whereabouts are not known. And I believe that you should go alone. Leave your man, Grayson, here with us. We shall find some way to employ him."

James frowned. "Why would I do that? He is useful to me."

Lydia lowered her voice to a whisper as she leaned across the table toward James. Despite the desperateness of the situation, he found himself admiring her long lashes and creamy skin. How he would miss stealing kisses, tasting the sweetness of her lips, inhaling the lavender scent of her hair, and diving into the intrigue of her eyes, eyes that were melted pools of dark chocolate. Whether sweet with laughter or dark with anger, they were always intriguing.

Now as she studied him, they were twin orbs of worry. "I do not think you should take Grayson because I do not trust him. How do you know he was not hired to kill you?"

James laughed. "With all the chances he has had, he has not done a very good job of it."

Lydia bristled. "Forcing you to London may be just the chance he needs."

"What about the fire?" asked Geoffrey.

"How do we know that he did not set it himself?" Lydia replied. "We have only his account of what occurred, and he did come out unscathed."

"And what of the rider?" Geoffrey persisted.

"Unless his cat can speak, we have only his word for that also," she replied.

Such doubts about the old sailor seemed ridiculous to James. Yet he knew that dismissing her suspicion too lightly would pique her ire. So he reined in his disregard and said, "You do raise an interesting possibility. However, I do not believe he is the sort of man to be bought by another. Grayson likes few men and respects even fewer. I do not believe he would debase himself for money, especially if it involved killing someone who treated him well."

"But can you be sure?"

"No. But, having commanded men, I have a feel for their natures. I have every confidence that I can trust the man."

Geoffrey gave a vigorous nod. "I agree with James. His man seems devoted. I believe it wise that James take him as a traveling companion."

Lydia wondered if her father simply did not want the man here. Either way, it seemed she was going to lose the argument. She could only hope that she had put enough suspicion into James' mind that he would be cautious and watchful of Grayson. The old sailor did not seem dangerous. Yet, at this point, she could not bring herself to trust anyone outside her house.

They finished breakfast, and all too quickly James was ready to depart. He and Grayson mounted their horses for the ride to the village and the hired coach that would take them to London.

Lydia clung to his arm as he stood beside his

horse. When he looked down into her face, she memorized the tiny lines etched beside his eyes, the small scar above his left eyebrow where a horse had kicked him, and the line of his firm jaw, shaved of the golden beard that matched his hair.

She could not bear it if something happened and he did not return. She wished she were the target instead of James and would willingly trade places with him. Was that how her mother had felt? Mariah had suspected the same sort of danger. Given the choice, Lydia believed she would still have given her life for Papa. She swallowed hard as she kissed James and watched him swing onto his horse. She longed to climb up behind him and share the danger. Yet she knew that neither James nor Papa would allow it. She would be forced to stay here and wait and hope that the killer revealed his hand before James returned. Yet what could possibly entice him to do so?

She watched them canter away and prayed they would be safe. She hoped desperately that Grayson would prove a trustworthy and loyal companion to James. It was a long way to London. There would be many opportunities for a traitor along the way.

She tried to ignore her fears as she watched the men disappear around the bend. They had fair weather for the trip. The storm had cleared, leaving the grounds blindingly white and glittering like a thousand tiny diamonds. The air smelled clean, washed by the snow, and everywhere the bare trees lay decorated with a soft dusting of white.

Christmas was not far away. As Lydia returned to the house, she determined to conquer her fears by engaging in a frenzy of gift-making for Papa, the servants, and James. She would knit gloves and scarves and warm woolen socks. And she would see to the planning of Christmas dinner. With luck, James would return well in time, and they would spend the day together, dining and exchanging gifts and roasting chestnuts upon the hearth.

And though her activities helped fill the time, Lydia found that the days passed slowly while he was away. More often than not she found herself plotting to draw out the would-be killer as she knitted or sewed or jotted down items for the Christmas menu.

On a particularly clear day in early December, after James had been away for two weeks, Lydia found that she could not tolerate another day spent inside the house. The snow had melted from the meadow, and she longed for a ride on her mare. As she felt sure the horse would be equally eager to escape the confines of the stable, she informed the butler of her plans and slipped away before Papa arose to object.

She had young Tom saddle her horse, and though she would have preferred to ride alone, she was too sensible to be so incautious. So, together, they set off across the meadow that lay behind the stable. The air was frosty and still. The winter sun bathed her face in light if not in warmth. Lydia drank in the intoxicating freedom of the miles of hills and fields that lay before her. Here in the country she was free from the manners and rules that dictated her behavior in society. As a schoolgirl she was never happier than when her rare visits home allowed her to fly pell-mell across the ground on the back of her horse, leaving thoughts of school far behind her.

Now, as she urged Dolly into a canter, she felt the same sense of freedom. As long as she could come out and taste and smell the magnificence of nature, she could stand to spend long evenings inside the house and wait for the days of spring when evening lingered and the scent of blossoms beckoned her to long walks in the gardens and rides upon the hills.

She decided to cross the road and make for the view gained from the western hill that overlooked the several cottages on the border of her father's land. She had often visited these cottages, bringing fresh bread and cheeses, had held the children in her lap and patted the heads of their friendly pets, dogs and cats who wanted the fragrant food in the basket nearly as much as did the children.

She smiled at the memory of those visits and vowed to go to each cottage before Christmas and bring cookies and muffins, rolled sausage and cheese.

These simple treats that she took for granted were great delicacies for the tenants. And it was this very realization that pricked her conscience into doing all that she could for people who paid rent wrought from rigorous and painstaking toiling in the ground.

She wanted to make their Christmas happy, as happy as she hoped her own would be. Yet only when James returned and the mystery was solved would she be totally content. As she sat her horse atop the rise, her thoughts drifted to a future Christmas. She imagined her family gathered around a tree that was alight with candles. The citrus aroma of punch and the spicy scent of sweetbreads filled with cinnamon and cloves would infuse the air. James and Papa, and perhaps a few little ones to tug at her skirts and ask how much longer they must wait, would complete her idea of perfect bliss.

She sat a while thus, breathing in the invigorating fresh air as she indulged her imagination with plans for the future. Tom complained not a word about the cold but sat his horse stoically behind his mistress and waited until the chill from the unsheltered height of the hill penetrated her bones and led her to turn her horse and head back toward home.

They descended the hill and crossed through a pretty park that, in his younger days, Papa had enjoyed tramping as he hunted for grouse. A little stream ran through it, and Lydia followed it, humming as she went. The alder and birch that grew along the banks gave them a measure of protection from the wind.

Her thoughts were still set upon the traditions and festivities of the coming Christmas season when they left the park to cross a grassy glen. Dolly high-stepped eagerly, knowing they were headed for a warm barn and a bucket of oats. Lydia patted her glossy neck and admired her sweet temper.

She was altogether taken by surprise by the sound of a shot ringing through the crisp air. Had they still been in the park, she would have believed a tenant had decided to fill his supper pot with deer or grouse. But they were out in the clearing. There was no game about, and no one had permission to hunt upon Papa's land.

She reined in her nervous mare and scanned the outskirts of the park. Surely it was unintentional, for James was not along, and all the attacks had been aimed at him. She turned to ask Tom if he had surmised the direction of the shot, only to see with horror what had befallen her groom. His jaw was clenched in pain. He pressed a gloved hand upon a spreading splotch of red that stained the shoulder of his coat.

Eyes wide with shock and confusion, he seemed not to understand what had happened to him. Yet Lydia understood at once. He had been shot, and it looked as though the bullet had passed through his shoulder. She glanced about, searching for help, but the only sign of human proximity had come from whoever had shot Tom. That being a most *un*comforting thought, she decided it in their best chance was to get away from the park as soon as possible.

She pulled Dolly beside Tom and asked, "Can you ride?"

He stared at here as though he did not understand.

"Here, you cling on, and let me take your reins. You have been shot, and we must get home."

She tried to keep the panic from her voice. But, in truth, it took all that she possessed to keep from flying across the meadow with the injured boy in a mad dash for the manor. She forced herself to lead the horses in a mild canter, for anything faster was sure to dislodge Tom from his saddle. As it was, the youth slipped unconscious when they crossed to the lane that led to town one way and to the manor the other.

The sickening thud of his sturdy young body hitting the ground stopped their progress toward home and help. Lydia gasped as she dismounted. How was she to get him home? She would never be able to lift him onto the horse, and the thought of leaving him in the road while she went for help seemed cruel.

As she was weighing her choices, she saw a rider coming down the road. She heaved a great sigh of relief and prayed that it would prove to be a sturdy young man come to help her. She waved her white kerchief as she waited for the well-bundled traveler to reach her. But when he did, she felt her blood chill as new doubt arose within her.

Reginald pulled up beside her, urging his massive bay to be still.

"Why, Lydia, whatever are you doing here in the road?"

She pushed aside her renewed suspicion. For him to help her with Tom was all that mattered now. She pointed to the boy lying motionless on the snowy lane.

"My groom has been shot. And now he has tumbled from his horse, and I have no way to get him home."

Reginald frowned deeply as he swung from his saddle. "Shot, you say?"

He knelt beside the boy and rolled him onto his back. "It looks as if the bullet has gone straight through, and he is losing a lot of blood. We must make haste to get the bleeding stopped."

He looked up at Lydia to say, "If I may borrow your handkerchief . . ."

"Yes, of course."

She handed it to him immediately, sorry only that she did not have a sturdier garment to stem the flow of blood from the wound. Reginald pressed the cloth inside Tom's coat. Leaving it in place, he scooped the boy into his arms and set him carefully atop the shoulders of the large bay. After he swung on behind, he said, "You lead his horse, and follow me to the manor."

He took off with a smooth canter, trying not to jounce Tom any more than necessary. Lydia took the reins of Tom's mount and followed upon Dolly. They arrived at nearly the same time. She watched as Reginald carried Tom to his room above the stables. When he was settled, Lydia gave orders to the hostler to go to the kitchen and fetch hot water before setting off for the village to fetch the doctor. In all the commotion, somehow the water arrived and the hostler was dispensed.

After all was quiet, she found herself alone in the small loft room, watching as Reginald peeled off the boy's coat and shirt and began to clean the wound. As she handed him bandaging, the renewed suspicions grew in her mind. Though he seemed truly sorry for the injury, how had he been so close upon the road at so near the time of the shooting? Could it be that he had shot Tom, thinking that he was James? Perhaps he had "happened" along to see if he had completed his ill task. She had not had a clear view of Reginald's face when he turned the boy over. She wondered if he had been dismayed not to see James. She intended to discover the answer and discover it soon.

Chapter Twelve

Reginald rocked back on his heels and shook his head. They had made young Tom as comfortable as possible, and there was nothing to do save wait for the doctor. The poor boy had long since lost consciousness. Fortunately, the compress they had fashioned for his shoulder had stemmed the bleeding.

He glanced at Lydia and said, "You have had a terrible shock. You should go back to the manor and rest. I will stay with the boy."

She shook her head. Though she had to lean against the small crude armoire to keep her knees from buckling, she was determined to stay. She felt responsible for Tom's injury and would not abandon him until she could be assured of his recovery. So she willed herself strength and bit her lip to keep it from trembling.

She supposed her disquiet was obvious when Reginald led her to the only chair in the tiny quarters and bade her sit. "You really should not insist upon staying, though I know it is no use to argue with you. In that regard, you remind me of Eve. Willful young women, the both of you."

Lydia would have uttered a tart reply regarding a comparison with Eve if she could have summoned the interest. As it was, her thoughts were centered upon Tom and the severity of his injury. He was so young. She could not stand the thought of his being maimed for life . . . or worse.

She forced herself to take a calming breath and asked, "Do you think he will live?"

Reginald regarded her with his hawklike gaze. Yet his eyes softened at the worry on her face, and he said, "He will live. He has lost a lot of blood, but he looks young and healthy, and it is only a wound to the shoulder. How did it happen?"

Lydia met his eyes with a candid stare. "That is exactly what I wish to know. I cannot believe this simple stable boy has any enemies so vile as to shoot him in the back. On the other hand, James has had more than one attempt made upon his life. It makes me wonder if someone presumed I was riding with James and shot this boy by mistake."

Reginald held her gaze unflinchingly. If he were

guilty, he showed no sign of it. And yet Lydia could not dismiss the coincidence of how he had come along so soon after the shooting.

She licked her dry lips and said, "Did you see anyone making an escape? You could not have been far from us when it happened."

He puckered his blond eyebrows. "I saw nothing of what occurred until I spied you on the road."

Lydia gave a slow nod. "I see. And may I ask what brought you along the road?"

"I was on my way to town."

She slanted a look at him from under her lashes. "I suppose you have no reason to wish harm to either Tom or James."

With a gritted jaw, he answered, "I see I am once again under suspicion. But I assure you, madam, I am a very good shot. Had I wanted to kill your man, I would not have hit his shoulder. And if you had been of a mind to notice, you would have seen that I carried no musket upon my horse, only a dueling pistol upon my person. I could hardly have hit the boy from much of a distance with that."

Lydia did not remember seeing a musket. Besides, that would be so easy to check that he dared not risk lying. So she sighed deeply and rested her chin on her hand. Reginald really had no motive other than his desire for her hand. And after all her accusations, she doubted he wanted her any longer.

"I am sorry. It is just that you were the only one

close by. I know you have no real reason to murder James."

Even though she had found Reginald an insufferable bore, she did not want to believe he was guilty. She hated to think that anyone she knew would attempt murder. It could only be a stranger, someone who wanted something from James. Suddenly the thought occurred to her that this could be wholly unconnected with the estate. What did she know of James' background in India? Perhaps someone held a grudge or had a debt against him that he had not paid.

She chewed her lip. The thought was disconcerting. If they were to be married, did she not have a right to know about ghosts from his past? It was a black mark indeed if he had not confided in her. And now he was off in London, and she could not even ask him.

Her thoughts were interrupted by Reginald's reply to her exoneration of his actions. His gaze softened as he said, "Of course you are distraught. It is only to be expected that a woman does not think clearly at such times. Nonetheless, I am relieved to be pardoned. May I assume that this pattern of accusation is ended?"

She bristled at his remark upon her gender yet was determined not to quarrel. She hadn't the energy, so she said, "I do not wish to accuse you. I wish only to know the truth of what is happening."

He patted her shoulder, and she resisted the urge to pull away. She had been ungracious, and now that he wished to console her, she must be civil. She was in his debt for his help with Tom. She shuddered to think what would have become of the boy if Reginald had not come along.

Because of that gratitude she accepted his company and counted the minutes until the doctor's carriage finally pulled up outside the stable and the stout man climbed the stairs to Tom's chamber. His round face was flushed with cold and exertion. Reluctantly Lydia left him with Reginald to examine Tom. Though she wanted desperately to help, all she could do was pace the length of the stables with the hostler, who carried an obvious fondness for Tom.

The doctor took his time, finally coming down to say, "The loss of blood is what has me worried. Nonetheless, if he remains still, I believe he has a good chance of recovery. He will need a nurse to stay with him."

Lydia nodded and swallowed over the lump in her throat. "Do you have someone in mind?"

"There is a woman in the village who sits with the sick. I could send her."

Lydia nodded. "I shall be here often as well. Is there anything else we might do to improve his chance of recovery?"

The doctor shook his head. "We have only to wait. Time will tell how he will fare."

The hostler stepped forward. "Begging your pardon, ma'am. I could move upstairs at night and stay with him."

Lydia nodded. "Thank you, Pete. That would ease my mind."

She turned to the doctor. "Would you care to come to the house for a glass of wine? I shall try to persuade Mr. Smyth to join us."

The doctor's round, crinkled face relaxed. "I could use a cup to face the chill going back to town."

Lydia led the way as the two men followed her to the house. Pete had gone up to be with Tom, and Lydia knew he would summon them at once if they were needed. And yet, she still could not shake the nagging feeling of guilt that had beset her. If she had not gone riding, Tom would not have been shot. And if she had questioned James more thoroughly as to his past deeds, she might have uncovered the reason and possibly the person responsible for the attacks.

For now, she would play the gracious hostess. But when James returned, she intended to have a long talk. And she would not be satisfied with anything save the truth.

She escorted the men to the drawing room, where Papa joined them all for a glass of wine. Lydia found it soothing to her nerves and was grateful for the relief. After the initial retelling of the events, the men took over the conversation, leaving her free to pursue her own thoughts. She wondered at how unreal it all seemed now. As she sat in the comfort of the overstuffed armchair watching the fire crackle in the familiar hearth, it was as though she had imagined the whole horrid morning. The next time she went to the stable, she would find Tom with a grin on his face, eager to assist her.

But she had not imagined it, any of it. As soon as her guests left, she planned to go back and sit with Tom. That would bring the reality of his circumstances crashing back down upon her. And she was heartily sorry for that.

In London, James jostled through the throng that milled about inside the men's club. He had enjoyed a fine supper and stimulating conversation. And now, at half-past midnight, he was weary and ready to go home. Perhaps he would be able to sleep deeply, untroubled by the dreams that had haunted him since he left Lydia. Every night he had searched for her in his sleep. Through gray fog and a cold mist he sought her until he would stumble upon her, lying upon the cold ground with barely a breath left in her body. And though he was not a superstitious man, he found the dreams unsettling.

He was weary from two weeks in London and more than ready to go home. Yet the time had not been wasted. He had replaced his wardrobe and that of Grayson. And though the crusty old sailor proclaimed the new clothes too fancy for his taste, James had seen him admiring himself in the tall looking glass on more than one occasion.

It was fortunate he had not let go his lease on the small house on Baker Street. It would serve him during what he hoped were rare trips to London. He preferred country life, but if he must come, he hoped to bring Lydia from now on. It would be pleasant to take in the theatre and then go out to a romantic dinner afterward.

Just the thought of Lydia made him long for her. This time apart had convinced him that he would rather face danger in the country than loneliness in the city. And yet, when he returned, there would be the next attempt on his life to worry about. And he knew it was just as terrible a strain on Lydia as it was on him.

So he had made an attempt to hire a detective. However, when he could find none who impressed him, he decided he must solve the plaguing mystery on his own. And when he did, he and Lydia would be free to enjoy their life together.

His trips to the pub had been useful in that he had learned of a cottage for lease only a few miles from his previous lodging. He was to make arrangements in the morning for the terms of lease. Then, within the week, he would pack his bags and return to Lydia. He would face the danger that awaited him, for he was sure that, given time, the shooter would reveal himself. Until then, it was his task to stay alive long enough to uncover the fiend.

Lydia was grateful for the steady recovery that Tom made each day. The doctor visited each afternoon and proclaimed no sign of infection. The woman from the village was dismissed from her duties now that Tom was allowed to sit up in bed. His spirits were good, especially when Lydia came. They played cards, and, though she knew he was in pain, he seemed not to notice when she assisted him with his hand.

Though profoundly thankful regarding Tom's recovery, she often felt overwhelmed by her anxiety over James. She knew that Tom believed the shooting was no more than an accident done by a poacher. And she had told him no differently, for she had no proof. Yet knowing that someone was out there, waiting for another chance, kept her heart and mind in a constant stew.

She missed James dreadfully. But she did not miss the fear for his safety she endured when he was present. And though she longed to delve into his past for the sake of finding an answer, she dared not wish for his return and the renewing of the fires and shooting.

Therefore, when he arrived, calling her name from the stable stairs, she was wholly unprepared for him. She excused herself from Tom and hurried to meet him upon the narrow flight. He caught her 'round the waist and hugged her to him.

"I have missed you, Lydia. I could not stay away any longer."

She melted into him, tears welling in her eyes as she pressed against his strong chest. As much as she feared for him, she could not deny her profound pleasure at his return. Every nerve in her body reacted to his warmth, the masculine scent that lingered from tobacco and ale, and the feeling of safety from being held in his arms.

After a moment, she realized that Grayson and the hostler were nearby. She blushed, sure that their sharp eyes missed nothing. And though she was not hiding her feelings for James, she had no desire to bandy them in front of the hired help.

"Would you like to go in and see Tom?" she asked.

James nodded. "The butler told me you were here with an injured stable boy. What happened?"

"My guess is that someone thought he was you."

James frowned. It was bad enough that someone had shot at him. But to have an innocent servant injured was not to be borne. He must find a way to end this foul business.

He entered the tiny room, hunching to keep from hitting his head against the rafters.

The boy struggled to rise, but James quickly said,

"Stay where you are. I have no wish to cause you more pain."

The boy's dark eyebrows rose quizzically, yet he sank gratefully back onto his elbows.

"How are you feeling?" James asked.

"Mending quickly, sir. Thanks to good nursing." The boy grinned a cheeky grin, and Lydia was glad to see that his spirits were in good form.

James nodded. "I am glad to hear it. If there is anything that I can do to make you more comfortable, I hope you will let me know."

"Thank you, sir. I will."

Lydia noted that Tom was looking fatigued from this interview with a gentleman and took James' arm. "Tom could use a rest. I am sure he is exhausted from beating me at cards. We should retire to the house and let Pete tend him for a while."

With a last nod at Tom, James allowed her to maneuver them toward the stairs. They trod down to let Pete know they were going to the house. Grayson stayed at the stable, happy to keep company with the hostler and talk his ear off at the same time.

Lydia shivered as they left the warmth of the stable. A cold north wind tugged at her muslin skirt and bit at her face and nose, making her breathe in short gasps. She clutched her shawl about her, struggling to keep it on her shoulders as she labored toward the back door and into the library.

They slipped inside and shoved closed the door. The wind growled in complaint, rattling the windows and pulsing against the door. They ignored its whining as they shed wraps and warmed themselves before the roaring fireplace.

The heat soon warmed Lydia's frozen cheeks and hands. She rang for tea, and they settled together upon the settee to speak of London until the tea arrived. Sarah brought it and then left when Lydia dismissed her, so that she might serve it herself. She caught her bottom lip as she performed the task, knowing that she was about to ask James the most important question of their relationship.

She glanced at his cheerful countenance and then plunged ahead. "I must know if there is something you are not telling me."

Frowning, he set down his cup. "What do you mean?"

"I cannot help but wonder why you are being targeted. Did you have a dispute with someone in India over a woman, gambling debts, or the like? I do not like to ask, but I feel that, if we are to be married, it is my right to know your past."

A flicker of hurt showed in his vivid blue eyes. Yet he took her hand and said, "I can assure you that I am concealing nothing from you. I have besmirched no woman's reputation nor made off with any money other than my own. My time in India was rather dull, and my service in the Navy was without scandal. I have no way to prove this, but I know no more than you about the reason for the attacks."

Looking into his face, Lydia could not believe that he had lied. He did not flinch from her question but looked steadily into her eyes. She gently squeezed his hand and said, "I could never marry a man who would keep a secret that put others in danger. I did not believe that you would do so, and I am fully convinced now that you have not. Still, I had to ask." She smiled apologetically.

He brushed a stray tendril from her cheek and said, "I could never keep a secret that would put you in danger. I long desperately to get to the bottom of this."

"As do I," she agreed. "Surely there is some way to draw out the assailant."

"I have spoken to Grayson, and we have agreed that he is to keep watch at night at our new residence and sleep during the day. He wants to do a bit of prowling around and see if he might catch someone sneaking near the place."

Lydia sighed. "I hope so. I will not rest easily until this is over."

James kissed the tip of her nose. "Neither will I. The house I have let is not far from here. Would you like to ride out and see it?"

Lydia shook her head. "I have had quite enough of riding with men who are targets for attack. I could not bear to have you shot right before my eyes. Can you not stay here tonight, safe in this house?"

"You need not worry. We have hired a coach from town to travel there. We will be safe inside if you will come with me. Then I will send you back in the coach."

Lydia sighed with relief. "Promise me you will not go out on horseback until you are safe."

"I shall not ride about unless I absolutely must."

Mesmerized by the concern in her dark eyes, he leaned down and kissed her, loving the velvet softness of her lips. He ran his long, tapered fingers along her neck and felt her shiver. How he longed to stay here with her as husband and wife, to kiss her beside this fire every night and have no reason to be parted.

Since he could not yet do so, he enjoyed their leisurely kiss before pulling her to her feet. "Come. I want to show you my new house."

"I hope this one does not burn down," Lydia said darkly.

"It will not. I am sure Grayson is an excellent watchman."

They sent for Grayson and wrapped themselves snugly against the wind. They hurried to the coach and piled inside, while Grayson rode atop with the driver. James sat beside Lydia and took her gloved hand in his own sturdy gloves and said, "I am glad Tom will recover. I do feel terrible about the lad. I meant what I said about letting me know if there is anything I can do for him."

She smiled. "I know. I long to discover who shot him. I was suspicious of your Grayson. Yet it makes no sense that he would burn down the house when he knew you were not home."

James nodded. "I am convinced that Grayson is devoted to me."

"Then who could it be?"

James shook his head. "I thought perhaps it was someone newly arrived in town. So I stopped into the pub before I came here and inquired as to whether there was anyone new about. It is hard to keep anything concealed from gossip at the pub." He laughed. "I was told the only one new here was me."

Lydia grimaced. "Well, you are certainly not trying to shoot yourself."

They rattled along, each lost in thought. Though the shades were pulled down tightly against the cold, the wicked wind drifted into the coach and chilled their bones. Lydia was more than ready to alight when they reached the new cottage where James would live.

She gave a quick glance to the hedges and gardens as he hustled her to the house. The entire grounds had the look of being overgrown. The lawn was covered with blown leaves, turned brown and sodden by the melted snow. Limp vines, overcome by the winter chill, clung to the house. Between the vines she spied the dismal gray slate of the house and two windows that peered out like unseeing eyes.

James hustled her to the front door that, when opened, gave a protesting squeak on its rusty hinges. She stepped into a hallway with fading rose wallpaper. A musty smell assailed her, and she wondered how long the house had been shut up.

James wrapped an arm around her shoulders. "I know it is cold. We have not had a chance to light a fire. I shall show you around quickly and bundle you back to the coach."

They took a quick tour of the kitchen and parlor and the two bedrooms that lay at the top of the stairs. In each room the ravages of time showed on furnishings and wallpaper. The floors were scuffed and covered with dust. It would never be a house Lydia would want to call home.

Keeping firmly to his promise, James did not let her linger but bundled her back to the coach, while Grayson brought in wood to start their fires. Though the house had left her with a sad impression, she smiled, keeping a brave front for James as she boarded the coach.

"Promise you will stay safe," she said.

He leaned in and kissed her tenderly. "I shall be fine."

He closed the door, and Lydia felt the coach lurch as it bore her away. She had no desire to look behind her at that gray, shrouded house. Something about it gave her an ill foreboding that she longed to escape.

She did not see or hear from James for two long days. At last a letter arrived inviting her to an early tea. Papa agreed that Tom would drive her in the old family coach, bringing her back before dark. Delighted, Lydia flew about, donning a green muslin day dress and drawing her hair into a topknot that Sarah adorned with a silk ribbon. She pulled on her warmest cloak and hurried out to board the coach that Pete had pulled to the front of the house.

In spite of her dislike of the run-down house, she could not wait to see James. By the time the coach rattled along the rutted lane to the house, Lydia was a bundle of eagerness. Her cheeks flamed with the assurance that he would embrace her and kiss her. She longed for the feel of his firm chest against her soft one, of strong arms to encircle her, and warm, passionate lips to drain the cold from her own.

Tom helped her down when they pulled to a stop. She wondered if James had improved the house since she had last seen it. Upon sight of it, she shook her head as a smile curved her lips. He was a man. How likely was he to tend to the fine details of his surroundings?

It was several moments before she heard answering footsteps to her knock at the door. James opened the door. For a moment he seemed taken aback.

Then he beamed down at her. His eyes lit with pleasure as he said, "My darling Lydia, what a surprise. I wanted to see you, but the weather has been so cold, I did not dare ask you to come."

As he stepped back to welcome her inside, Lydia felt her mind churn in confusion. Why should he be surprised to see her? Surely in her eagerness to see him, she had not misread the note. It had clearly stated that she was invited today for afternoon tea.

She allowed him to take her wrap and deposit it upon the coatrack. Then she asked, "Did you not expect me? I received a note this morning inviting me to tea."

James stared at her as though she had gone a bit daft. "I did not send 'round a note. Perhaps it was from another friend. Eve, perhaps?"

Lydia shook her head. "No. It clearly stated the time and place."

He frowned. "How odd."

Then, growing playful, he pulled her close and said, "Are you sure you did not read what you wished to see? Perhaps you wanted to come here as much as I wanted to see you."

She pushed aside the questions in her mind and smiled up at him. "I did wish to see you."

"Just as I thought," he murmured, as he lowered his head to kiss the color back into her lips.

They were locked in a warming embrace when another knock sounded on the door. James released

her reluctantly and turned about to see who was interrupting their private interlude. Lydia looked past
him to see that Eve stood upon the stoop, clutching
a worn velvet shawl about her shoulders.

"Ah, this makes sense," James said. "It is just as I
thought. You invited Lydia and have come to discover why she did not arrive."

He invited her in from the cold and chuckled. "I
am afraid she misread the invitation and came here
instead. But, no matter, I shall set the teakettle to
boil, and we shall all have tea."

He froze in midturn as Eve drew a pistol from the
folds of her shawl. She fixed him with a cold stare
that froze Lydia's blood as she took a step back and
aimed the pistol at them.

Her smile cynical, she said, "Is this not cozy, this
little party I have planned? I sent Lydia the invitation. I knew she would come scurrying right away
like a little mouse. It is too bad she will be caught in
the trap with the cat."

James took a step forward, and Eve cocked the
pistol. "Shall you hurry your death? This time I do
not intend to miss."

Her words stopped him. "*You* shot at me?"

"Indeed. For you see, with you out of the way, Reginald would become the rightful heir to the estate. My
grandfather was murdered, leaving only a daughter.
My mother grew up with the knowledge that the estate was stolen from her family. Her mother died

from the bitterness of the blow, and my mother never forgot. She tried to right things by killing Geoffrey, but she failed. And though it was our secret, she was consumed by guilt over your mother. Still, she never forgot the betrayal, and she taught me not to forget either."

Lydia felt weak-kneed with shock. She had known that Eve could be cunning, but she had never expected that she could be enticed toward murder. And to think that she was the one who had told Eve all about James' coming and how he was to inherit the estate. She turned to plead with Eve, desperate to stop her.

"You cannot mean to do this. You would be hanged for murder. Reginald would never want that."

"Not if there are no witnesses. I shall see that you are all in the house when it burns down this time. I am sorry to include you, Lydia, for I do hold some fondness for you. I tried to save you by matching you with Reginald. But you were too foolish to comply. Married to him, you would have kept your life and the estate. But now . . ."

"Please, Eve, you cannot do this."

James' narrow gaze rested upon the tall blond girl. "You cannot shoot us both. You have only one shot."

"Not true."

Eve produced the matching pistol in her other

hand. "I shall shoot you first and then Lydia. I will have time to reload before killing your man."

She gestured with the pistols. "Move to the kitchen. And, remember, I shall be right behind you."

When they had nearly reached the doorway, the front door burst open, and Reginald stepped inside. He strode toward his sister. "Hand me the pistols, Eve."

"No!"

She raised the gun to fire at James. Before Lydia could blink, Reginald drew a pistol from his coat and shot the gun neatly from her hand. Stunned by the force of the bullet, Eve shrank back with a cry. In two steps Reginald reached her and pried the other pistol from her hand.

Eve sank to the floor with a moan. Ignoring the others, her brother knelt beside her. "I was suspicious when you rode off alone again, and this time I followed you. Why, Eve, why would you do this?"

She began to rock and cry. "It was all for you. I wanted you to inherit the estate."

Reginald stood up, squarely facing James and Lydia. "I never wanted this. I had no idea she had gone so far. She showed me your family Bible and the line of inheritance, and we learned that I would inherit if not for James. Yet I never would have agreed to hasten that happening."

He shook his head and continued. "We came

here because Eve longed to return to our roots. Fortunately, she is not a marksman. She never had the patience to learn. But when I saw through your window that she was aiming at you, I was afraid she would maim or kill one of you by pure chance."

"Thank goodness you came along when you did," Lydia said.

Reginald's eyes locked on James, and for the first time Lydia saw the family resemblance. Though Reginald was pale like a ghostly shadow, like a wraith from the underworld compared to James, their blue eyes were unmistakably alike, as were their blond hair and tall height.

"I pray, sir, that you will not turn her over to the authorities. I shall not let her out of my sight. I promise we will move far away—to India, perhaps—and never trouble you again," Reginald promised.

James stared down at Eve. "How could we have peace knowing this may never end? Should you marry, she will poison your children toward us."

"I shall give her no opportunity to do so."

James nodded. "Then be on your way. I shall expect you to quit the village for London by the end of the week. I am taking your word that you will leave the country."

"You have my word upon it."

Lydia watched in silence as Reginald coaxed Eve to her feet, speaking as a parent to a child. "Come along now. You have behaved badly. And now we will both pay the price."

Eve did not meet their eyes. She slumped as she allowed Reginald to lead her to the door. After a few minutes they heard the sound of the horses clopping away along the drive.

Lydia was overcome by shivers. Now that it was over, she felt strangely light-headed.

"I think you must sit down," James told her.

She glanced at him to see that he, too, was unusually pale.

Once upon the settee, she said, "I think Reginald's explanation was overly generous to Eve. She did it for herself, not for him."

"Either way, it is over now. They will soon be far away."

He paused a moment and said, "I wonder that your father never told you of his niece and nephew.

"I suppose he thought it was for the best."

They sat together for some time with James holding her close until her violent shivers ceased. He looked tenderly into her eyes and said, "We have struggled dearly for our life together, and it will be worth every bit of strain that Eve has heaped upon us."

She smiled up at him. "Nonetheless, I am glad the mystery is over."

Grayson trod down the stairs and said, "Beggin'

your pardon. Thought I would go out and keep watch for a bit. Don't want trouble catchin' me sleepin'."

James and Lydia laughed.

"First, put on water for tea, and we shall tell you a story," James said.

Grayson tramped to the kitchen.

"I'll love you forever," James said.

Turning a radiant smile upon him, Lydia replied, "I love you too."

She snuggled next to him and knew, now that the curse was behind them, that the secret of the manor had been finally been put to rest.

Epilogue

September 30, 1815

A message from India to Mr. James Summers and Mrs. James Summers:

> *I am sorry to say that my sister died on the voyage to India. I hope that you will not remember her too unkindly. I shall stay on here and continue trade as a merchant. I wish you both health and happiness.*
>
> *Reginald Smyth*

Lydia turned the message over in her hands and felt tears well in her eyes. Poor Eve, beautiful and yet so bitter. Perhaps she would have been happy in India. Yet somehow Lydia had believed she would not. She was obsessed with the estate, and nothing would ever have taken its place. Now that she was free of it, perhaps she would finally rest in peace.

Lydia set down the letter and hoped fervently that it was so.